Lao Ti instinctively lunged to one side

She felt the sting of lead burrowing into her thigh, hips and midsection as she went down. Almost immediately she lost all feeling in her legs.

The assault rifle had fallen beyond her reach, and she doubted she could crawl to it in time to use the weapon against her assailant. She could hear the sound of footsteps crunching through the snow toward her. Closing her eyes, Lao tried to blot out the sensation of burning pain that raged through her and tried instead to concentrate on slowing her pulse. Her only chance for life at this point was to pass herself off as dead.

The footsteps stopped a few yards away where the cop was lying, and then there was one cracking sound that she deduced was a bullet slamming its way through the officer's skull, ensuring that he was indeed dead.

A twig snapped just off to her left, and Lao Ti knew that in a matter of seconds she would be next. She knew she was about to die.

Mack Bolan's

ABLE TEAM®

ABLE TEAM.

CLEAR SHOT

Dick Stivers

A GOLD EAGLE BOOK FROM
WORLDWIDE.

TORONTO • NEW YORK • LONDON • PARIS
AMSTERDAM • STOCKHOLM • HAMBURG
ATHENS • MILAN • TOKYO • SYDNEY

First edition February 1988

ISBN 0-373-61234-6

Special thanks and acknowledgment to
Ron Renauld for his contribution to this work.

Printed in Canada

PROLOGUE

Daylight crept through shutter slats and fell across the bed, rousing Nan Felsur from the deep sleep that had finally claimed her after the long trip to Wyoming. She was in a guest room just down the hall from the kitchen, and she awoke to the smell of coffee, sourdough pancakes and bacon, which she heard sizzling and snapping in the cast-iron skillet. The sounds and smells brought back memories of happier times back home in Cincinnati, years ago, before things had started to go wrong for her. It seemed appropriate that she should be greeted by such familiar, reassuring sensations her first day in Wyoming. It had to be an omen of good things to come.

She sat up in bed and pulled the down comforter tightly around her to ward off the room's chill. As she watched specks of dust dancing in the golden glow of a shaft of light, she heard voices in the kitchen. Men. Rudy, no doubt. And Jimbo and Sam. Claudette had introduced her to them last night, shortly after they had arrived at the ranch. Part of the film crew. They were probably planning the day's shooting.

It had been a long night for Nan. Before succumbing to sleep, she had spent hours tossing and turning, her mind alive with excitement and anticipation. Today the filming would begin. Her dreams would begin to come true. It hardly seemed possible. Was it really only four days ago that she had been roaming penniless down Hollywood's side streets, just one of hundreds of teenage runaways trapped in the web of harsh reality that lay beneath that city's tinsel glitter? No, that had to be a lifetime ago, she thought. Those hard times were far behind her, and she would no longer have to dwell on them, unless a movie magazine reporter wanted to know about her life before she was discovered.

There was a soft knock on her door.

"Yes?" she called out.

The door opened. A man in his early forties peered in, a glimmer in his gray eyes. He was dressed head to toe in faded denim, and his ruddy skin was equally weathered by exposure to the elements. A curl of sandy hair hung across his forehead below the wide brim of his felt hat.

"Up and at 'em, sweetcakes," he told her. "Got a big day ahead of you."

"I'll be right there, Rudy," Nan promised.

Rudy nodded and left the girl alone. Nan threw off the covers and hurriedly changed from her flannel nightgown into the new corduroy slacks and knit sweater Claudette had bought for her before they'd left Los Angeles. Opening the shutters, the young woman let sunlight wash over her as she stared out at a magnificent view of the Wind River range, a chunk of pristine Wyoming wilderness southeast of Grand Teton and Yellowstone National Park. There was snow above the timberline, crowning distant Whiskey Mountain and Union Peak in brilliant whites. Nan had always hated winter in the Midwest, but here the season seemed glorious and majestic. She felt glad to be alive.

A hearty breakfast with the three-man film crew helped buoy her spirits further. She laughed along as Rudy and the man next to him teased her about her upcoming screen debut. Nan knew they were just trying to keep her from becoming too nervous.

"Yeah, Madonna's gonna be quakin' in her boots once she sees ol' Nan here on the screen, right, Jimbo?" Rudy said, winking at his companion.

"You bet," Jimbo agreed. He was a big man, six-two and two hundred pounds in his coveralls and cowboy boots, elbows propped on the rough-hewn table that took up most of the cramped dining room. The whole ranch house had a similar feel—rustic and small. "She'll be damn sorry she turned down the part, and that's a fact."

"Oh, come on," Nan said. "Madonna wasn't offered my part."

Jimbo shrugged his shoulders and swilled down the last of his coffee. "If you say so," he told the teenager.

The third man, a lean figure wearing a down vest over his Pendleton shirt, sat apart from the others and didn't join in the conversation. He smoked a cigarette as he tinkered with a bulky industrial-size video camera, cleaning the lens and making sure its controls were in working order. From time to time he casually glanced through his smoke at Nan and the other two men. There was a detached coldness in his dark eyes. Nan met his gaze once and quickly looked away. He hadn't spoken the night before, either, and something about him made her uneasy. She wished that someone else worked the camera. But she wasn't about to start making demands. At least not this soon in her career.

Rudy finished his bacon, then checked his watch and rose from the table. "We best get to the barn or Claudette's gonna be after our hides."

"You know all your lines?" Jimbo asked Nan as they left the table and bundled up for the walk outside.

Nan nodded, grabbing the script she felt was a blueprint for her first step on the road to cinematic immortality. "It's not like I really have that much to say."

"Well, maybe next film, right?" Rudy held Nan's coat while she slipped her arms through the sleeves.

"Yep. This is just a start."

"Let's move it, Sam!" Jimbo called out to the camera-man, who had yet to leave the table.

Sam slowly stubbed out his cigarette and eyed Jimbo and Rudy. Smoke trailed from his nostrils. He said nothing, but got up from the table, camera tucked under his arm, and started for the door. Nan was the first one out, but she could hear a few words exchanged behind her back.

"You tryin' to spook her or what?" Rudy hissed at the cameraman.

"Outta my face," Sam growled. He had a deep, thick voice. "I don't play your games."

"Shut up, both of you," Jimbo snapped.

Nan pretended not to hear the argument. She'd been told how temperamental Hollywood people could be, and she wasn't about to let a few rough edges spoil her enjoyment of her first performance.

A stiff breeze whipped across the ranch. Nan turned up the collar of her jacket and leaned to one side, putting her shoulder to the wind. The ground was hard under their feet as they strode quickly toward the barn, located a hundred yards away. Off to their right, a few head of cattle grazed on the other side of an old wooden fence that was in need of major repairs. A thin gravel driveway wound its way into the pines that surrounded the ranch, leaving it closed off from the main road some two thousand yards away.

Rudy told her that outlaws had once frequented this part of Wyoming, seeking refuge from the law after robbing banks or raiding stagecoaches or freight trains down in the lowlands, near towns like Riverton and Lander and Tipton. Butch Cassidy's Wild Bunch, Kid Curry, Isom Dart, Big Nose George Parrott, Tom Horn—a wealth of colorful figures from the past—had roamed this region, painting legends for themselves with the blood of their victims. The ranch itself, so old and remote, had probably served as a

hideout or way station for some of those same despera-
does.

Not surprisingly, the movie they were about to film was a
western set at the turn of the century. Nan was to play a
farmer's daughter who falls in love with the wounded bank
robber she helps nurture back to health after he shows up at
her father's ranch. It was a small role, Claudette had told
her, since the robber decides that he can't settle down and
leaves the ranch after only a few scenes with the farmer's
daughter. But it was a big opportunity, and Nan was determined to make the best of it.

Next to the barn was a circular corral, in the middle of
which blazed an untended campfire. Branding irons were set
over the flames, and Nan could see the forged iron turning
red and then white as it absorbed the heat.

"Got a few new calves to brand," Jimbo told her.

"Could I watch?"

"Don't flub your lines and we'll see, okay?"

Although the barn's exterior was hungry for a coat of
paint after decades of neglect, the interior was another story.
After passing through the main entrance, Nan and the three
men walked down a carpeted, paneled hallway that looked
as if it was part of a modern-day office building. Doorways
on either side of the corridor led to offices, editing rooms
and film processing labs used by the independent movie-
makers.

"I don't believe it!" Nan exclaimed, taking in the facilities for the first time. "It's like Hollywood out in the middle of nowhere!"

"Something like that." Jimbo led them through an arch-
way into a run-down stable that looked as if it was the only
remaining part of the original building. Hay was strewn on
the dirt floor and cows were in the stalls, contributing their
bovine scent to the distinct farm aroma. The only conces-
sions to modern times were thick electrical cords that curved

across the straw like snakes toward a set of film lights and a small sound system resting on a card table in one of the vacant stalls.

Claudette Simms was fussing over the scenery, lost in her directional duties. She was forty years old; a tall, angular woman wearing an oversize alpaca jacket and wide slacks tucked into a pair of ostrich-skin boots. She wore a Stetson over her straight auburn hair, and had eyes as green as clover.

"Ah, there's our little starlet," she said cheerfully when she spotted Nan. "Are we ready?"

Nan laughed nervously. "As ready as I'll ever be."

"Good, good."

Referring to her copy of the script, Claudette blocked out the first scene, which involved Nan milking a cow as the bank robber straggles into the barn. In the background, the three men readied the camera, lights and sound equipment, working with quiet efficiency. The rising sun poured light through cracks in the barn wall, forcing the group to rearrange the scene slightly.

When everything was ready, Nan was sent off into one of the side rooms to change into a period costume. It was a white cotton dress, low-cut and tight-fitting. When she returned to the stable, shivering from the cold, she asked Claudette, "Is this really something a farmer's daughter would wear to milk cows?"

Claudette smiled indulgently. "Well, maybe not, but we're allowed to take a little dramatic license. Besides, the movie really takes place during the summer, so the cotton won't seem that much out of place."

"But it's so cold I can see my breath!" Nan exclaimed.

The older woman sighed and moved away from the stall where a heifer was busy feeding at a trough full of hay. She rested a hand on Nan's shoulder. "Now, hon, if you expect to make your mark in show business, you're going to have to learn to do things the way you're told, okay?''

Nan could sense impatience in Claudette's voice, and immediately regretted her second-guessing. "You're right," she apologized. "Sorry."

"Okay, then," Claudette said, gesturing toward a short three-legged milking stool and wooden bucket that sat next to the heifer. "Let's get ready to give it your best shot, hmmm?''

Nan nodded and pulled in the folds of her skirt as she eased herself down onto the stool. It was an awkward position, but she did her best to look graceful. She was glad for the heat of the lights that glared down on her as she glanced back at Claudette, who had taken up position behind the video camera, which was now mounted on a tripod. For the first time, she noticed that Rudy, Jimbo and Sam were nowhere around.

"Where did the men go?"

"I figured the fewer people around the less nervous you'd be," Claudette told her.

"Thanks," Nan said appreciatively.

Claudette peered through the viewfinder and panned the camera slightly to her right, reframing the shot. "Okay, Nan. Start milking, just like I showed you. Remember, don't look at the camera...."

Nan nodded and drew in a deep breath.

"Action," Claudette yelled.

Hearing the soft whir of the camera, Nan leaned forward on the stool and reached for one of the cow's udders, fighting back her embarrassment at the feel of her fingers around the long, round knob of flesh. She could feel herself blushing as she squeezed with a slight tugging motion to draw milk. Think of your lines, Nan. Think about the stranger.

She hadn't even met the man playing the part of the robber. Claudette had suggested that Nan would do a better job of reacting to the man's unexpected arrival if she wasn't sure who to expect. For a moment the teenager found herself fantasizing that a big star was playing the robber and that Claudette had been withholding his identity so that Nan wouldn't be intimidated. What if it's Tom Cruise or Sean Penn? Nan thought.

"My, my, but she sure knows how to squeeze that thing, don't she?"

Nan was surprised to hear Jimbo, especially since his dialogue bore no resemblance to the robber's lines in her script. Confused, she turned slightly on the milking stool and looked in the direction of the man's voice.

"I got a little something you can take hold of, too," Jimbo drawled as he crossed the stable to leer down at Nan. Rudy and Sam flanked him on either side, and all three men wore expressions of wanton lust. Jimbo had a Colt .45 revolver in one hand and was fidgeting with his belt buckle with the other. Rudy carried a length of rope, while Sam clutched one of the branding irons, which still glowed with white heat.

"What are you doing?" Nan stood up and backed away from the men, knocking over the stool. "Stop it! This isn't funny!"

"Ain't supposed to be funny, bitch," Rudy said, taking a long stride and grabbing hold of the girl. "Just fun."

"You're hurting me!" Nan struggled to break free of Rudy's grasp, but he was too strong. Jimbo helped hold her still while Rudy began tying her hands behind her back. The girl looked past her tormentors toward Claudette. "Make them stop! Please, make them stop!" she pleaded.

But Claudette Simms had no intention of intervening, just as she had no intention of filming a movie about a farmer's daughter who falls in love with a wounded robber. As the three men overpowered Nan Felsur and began subjecting her to brutal sexual abuse, Claudette calmly remained behind the camera, recording the crime on videotape. Nan screamed, at first in fear and then in pain, and the sound system faithfully recorded her cries. The farm was miles from anyone who might overhear the screams, and even if by a fluke someone was closer and willing to investigate, he would be told that a movie was being made and that all the yelling was merely part of the performance.

The degradations that Nan Felsur suffered in front of Claudette Simms's camera went beyond pornography. Although Claudette dabbled occasionally in the market, she had recruited the teenager for a more sordid enterprise. The abuse and the torture were only preliminaries to the climax of this special kind of movie, a kind of movie that catered to a very specialized clientele.

Nan Felsur's first and last screen performance was in a snuff film, and by the time the camera stopped rolling her corpse had been branded and ravaged beyond recognition. Only her face had been spared the brunt of the three men's grisly brutality, although even in death her expression betrayed unfathomable pain and agony.

There was something special about that face, and it had nothing to do with the fact Nan Felsur was, or had been, photogenic. Claudette Simms had filmed the murders of far prettier girls. It had to do with who Nan Felsur was. When the man had pointed Nan out to Claudette only two days ago in Hollywood, his instructions to her had been specific.

Leave the face intact.

Claudette hadn't asked for reasons. She never did. That wasn't her concern. It was her business to film the deaths of young girls in enough graphic detail that they earned top dollar on the snuff circuit. And as she stopped the camera following the execution of her latest victim, Claudette coolly congratulated herself on another job well done.

Sweating from the exertion of their performances, the three men left Nan's mangled body in the stall and staggered away, strangely silent. Rudy and Jimbo wore blank expressions on their faces. Sam, however, had his lips twisted into a self-satisfied smirk. He idly twirled the bloodied cattle brand as if it was a baton. He was the first to the doorway, but before he could reach the latch the door swung inward and a fourth man strode into the enclosure.

"She's all yours," Sam told the newcomer, cracking a grin. "Sloppy seconds."

Dave X. Fabyan was five foot five and wore a five-hundred-dollar sharkskin suit. He held the door open until the other men had left, then strode over to view the remains of Nan Felsur. He was the same man who had marked her for death, and he casually lit a filterless cigarette as he stared at the body.

"You'll like this one," Claudette promised the man in the suit as she patted the camera.

"I'm sure I will," Fabyan said. "And I'm glad you're finished, because I have a new project for you...."

1

Rosario Blancanales figured superficial bullet wounds were like out-of-town relatives dropping by unexpectedly. Some were an absolute nuisance, taking up all your time and attention and bringing you nothing but grief; others were only a minor inconvenience and even provided a blessing of sorts by forcing you to take time out from your daily grind for some much-needed diversion. The slow-healing puncture in his right thigh, received during a recent skirmish with gun-runners in New Orleans, ranked somewhere between the two extremes. The wound was bothersome enough that Hal Brognola had finally ordered Blancanales to take some time off from Stony Man antiterrorist operations, but faced with the prospect of an extended period of rest and relaxation, the hyperactive Hispanic was far from elated. His idea of a vacation was sleeping in one day a week.

But orders were orders, so Blancanales had reluctantly packed a few belongings and left behind the harsh cold of a Virginia winter for sunnier climes on the West Coast. Like the bullet that had put him out of commission, he was playing the part of visiting relative. Unlike the projectile, however, he had called ahead to let his family know he was coming. As he limped from the arrivals lounge of the L.A. International terminal, Blancanales scanned the crowd on the other side of the security barricade for a familiar face.

"'Ey, Rosie, *brolo*!"

Blancanales turned, trying to track down the unmistakably cheerful voice of his kid sister. In his mind he held the image of a gangly, awkward teenager with braces and pigtails that did a lousy job of concealing her oversize ears. What he saw was something else.

A young woman pushed her way through the throng and smiled at her brother, showing straight, braceless teeth. Her hair was teased and full-flowing, draped across the padded shoulders of her Anne Taylor blouse. Gone was the uncertain clumsiness of puberty, replaced by a poise and self-confidence that instantly reminded Blancanales of his mother. She wore makeup that made her look even older than her eighteen years.

"Pixie?" Blancanales muttered in disbelief. "Is that you?"

The girl laughed, "Nobody calls me Pixie anymore."

"I can see why. Maria, you've grown up on me."

"That's what you get from staying away so long, Rosie," Maria taunted good-naturedly.

"Nobody calls *me* Rosie anymore," Blancanales told her as they broke away from the crowd. He was traveling light, carrying all his goods in a shoulder tote so they wouldn't have to bother with the mob at baggage claims.

"What *do* they call you?"

"A lot of things," Blancanales confessed. "Mostly, though, they call me Pol. Short for Politician."

Maria frowned. "Don't tell me you're in politics now."

"Not exactly," Pol told her with the winning smile that was the real source of his nickname. "But let's not talk about me, okay?"

"Right," Maria sighed, shaking her head with obvious frustration. "Still Mr. Top Secret, huh?"

"Afraid so, Sis."

Like fellow Able Team members Carl Lyons and Gadgets Schwarz, Blancanales was not at liberty to divulge his membership in one of the country's most sensitive special forces. It wasn't only because of the nature of their assignments, which of necessity usually entailed activities beyond the bounds of legal recourse. Nor was it strictly because of fear of reprisal by congressional watchdogs or left-wing media piranhas eager to feed on the next covert operative to be caught with his charter down. The way Pol saw it, the less he revealed about his unique role in dealing with the increasingly complicated world of urban terrorism, the less likely his family and acquaintances were to be dragged into it. Coming from a family as large as his, it was a major consideration.

"You've changed, too, you know," Maria told her brother as they waited for the pedestrian traffic light. She reached up and tousled Pol's prematurely graying hair. "You're starting to look more like Poppa than Poppa."

Pol groaned. "Thanks, I needed that."

His hair might have aged, but Blancanales had retained much of the powerful physique he'd had as far back as his stint in Nam more than twenty years before. Firm muscles wrapped themselves around his large-boned frame, and the weight of his tote bag was negligible in his meaty hand.

When the light changed, Maria led her brother to the nearest parking structure and past rows of cars to an antiquated Volkswagen Beetle that looked to be on its fifth paint job and its sixth reincarnation. Despite the new color and updated bumper stickers, Blancanales instantly recognized the vehicle.

"Madre de Dios!" he exclaimed. *"La Cucaracha!"*

The Beetle—or "the Cockroach," as Pol called it—had been Blancanales's first car, bought secondhand by his immigrant father as Pol's high school graduation present. He had gone through numerous adolescent rites of passage in the vehicle prior to enlisting in the Army shortly after his eighteenth birthday. The Volkswagen had stayed in the family, put to use by his other brothers and sisters over the years.

"I take good care of it," Maria assured Pol as they got in and she started up the engine. "She still has a few miles left in her."

"I guess she does at that!" Pol beamed as they pulled out of the lot and headed for the freeway. Although Blancanales had grown up in the East Los Angeles barrio and the border town of San Ysidro, two hours south of the airport, his parents now resided up north in the San Fernando Valley, a sprawl of interconnected communities on the other side of the Santa Monica Mountains. A million and a half people called the Valley home, and during what passed for the rainy season in Southern California it was almost an inviting location. The surrounding hills were green, and with the smog held at bay by recent rains you could actually see them most of the time.

As they cleared Sepulveda Pass and turned onto the Ventura Freeway, Maria brought Pol up-to-date on the family. Hector and José were in Chattanooga, Tennessee, of all places, running a successful auto repair shop. Toni, as Pol knew, was still a security consultant with Able Group. Roberto, the youngest, was living at home and setting scoring records as a point guard at Canoga High School. And she had plans to move into an apartment near Pierce Community College, where she was taking acting lessons.

"Acting?" Blancanales mused as they took the Canoga exit and headed north to the West Valley barrio.

"Yeah, why not?" Maria said. "I'm going to be the Rita Moreno of the eighties . . . or at least the nineties."

Blancanales reached over and jabbed his sister lightly on the shoulder. "Go for it, kid."

"I plan to."

Warner Center was fast becoming an urban hub for that section of the Valley, with high rises pulling in increased business activity and driving up housing prices in the surrounding neighborhoods. Improvements were even being made in pockets of Canoga Park that had long been known for their levels of crime and poverty. Jorges and Anna Blancanales had bought their home in the center of a neighborhood undergoing revitalization, and Maria pulled to a stop in front of a well-groomed lawn that reached back to a freshly painted two-story house. Anna, a stocky, feisty woman in her midfifties, looked up from her weeding and let out a gasp of joy when she saw her son get out of the Volkswagen.

"Jorges!" she called out as she rose to her feet. "Jorges! Come, Rosario's home!"

The family patriarch emerged from the side yard, holding a pair of hedge shears. Like his son's, Jorge's hair was graying, but it was also much thinner. He smiled broadly and set the shears aside as he stepped forward and waited for his turn to embrace the younger man.

"Hey, Pops," Pol said as they hugged, "nice digs you got here."

Jorges shrugged. "It's a home, but I'd trade it all to have you brats running around in diapers again. We don't see enough of you, Rosario."

"You're limping!" Anna cried, staring at Pol's sore leg.

"Just an excuse to see you," Pol insisted. He gestured toward the house. "How about a quick tour? Then I want to eat tamales until I can't move...."

ANNA BLANCANALES HADN'T LOST her cooking touch, and after less than a day at home Pol was, in fact, nearly immobilized by his appreciation of his mother's culinary prowess. Besides tamales, he'd sampled frijoles, burritos, *carnitas*, crabmeat enchiladas and freshly made tortilla chips that went down easily with *cerveza*. And that had just been supper.

Somehow he managed to sleep through the mutinous turmoil in his belly, but come morning he couldn't bring himself to tackle a plateful of *huevos rancheros*. He opted for juice out on the back porch, where he watched from the sidelines as Roberto shot baskets in the driveway, demonstrating his ball-handling finesse between jumpers and driving lay-ups.

The elder Blancanales pulled up a seat next to his son and patted Pol's uninjured thigh. "So, you can stay for a while this time?"

"Maybe a few days," Pol replied, catching a pass from Roberto and then tossing it back toward the basket so that his brother could practice rebounding.

"Your mother worries about you."

"Pops, don't start—"

"She wears out rosaries praying that you will be okay." Jorges jabbed a finger at his son's bullet wound, forcing Pol to wince. "Maybe that was God trying to tap you on the shoulder to get your attention, only you were moving around too much and he missed."

Pol smiled wryly as he glanced down at his thigh. It sure as hell hadn't been God down in New Orleans firing lead his way, and if he hadn't been moving the bullet would have tapped something more crucial than his shoulder. He wanted to tell his father as much, but even if he wasn't sworn to secrecy, Pol knew better than to egg the old man on. They'd locked horns many times when Pol was growing up, and both men knew that it wouldn't take much of a provocation for them to fall back into their old ways. For Anna's sake, they had long ago called a truce.

"But I am lecturing, eh, Rosario?" Jorges chuckled, guessing his son's thoughts. "Very well. No more of this talk. I know you must keep your secrets and do what you feel is right. Just be careful. For your mother's sake."

Pol nodded and set up Roberto for another rebound. Maria left the house through the side door and started for the Volkswagen parked at the head of the driveway. She waved over her shoulder at Jorges and Pol.

"Off to class," she told them. "Shakespeare."

"Break a leg," Pol called out.

As he watched his daughter back out into the street and drive off, Jorges sighed with nostalgia. "Ah, she is the second coming of her mother. Our little treasure."

"She sure is something," Pol agreed.

Transitory as his life-style had been over the years since he'd first left home, Pol had always used his folks' address as his official residence. Every few weeks his mail was lumped together and sent on to a post office in Washington, D.C., and from there it eventually backtracked to the Stony Man compound in Virginia's Blue Ridge Mountains. As it turned out, there was a load that his parents had been readying to send when he'd called about his visit, and once Jorges went off to finish the hedges and Roberto concluded his basketball clinic so he could get to school, Pol started sorting through the envelopes, looking for any correspondence of interest.

Halfway through the pile was a newsletter called *Grunt*, which chronicled the postwar activities of Vietnam vets, particularly those who'd done time on the front line. As an Army volunteer who'd proven himself in basic training and then at jungle warfare and jump schools as a member of the elite Special Forces, Blancanales had met a lot of soldiers, most of them youths like himself, forced to grow up in a hurry. A good number of those acquaintances had come back to the States in a box, often in pieces. Others, like Pol, had come through the hellfire with only scars and bad memories to contend with. Not surprisingly, there was a strong camaraderie among those who had risked their lives in Nam, and newsletters like *Grunt* and a few dozen others proved a valuable means by which the veterans could stay in touch with one another.

As a case in point, when Pol skimmed through the newsletter a name from his past jumped out at him, and he murmured, "Pete Banfield. I'll be damned...."

"What's that, son?" Jorges queried from across the yard.

"Some guy I went through basic training with runs a survivalist store here in the Valley." He read off an address on Sherman Way in Reseda and asked his father how close it was.

"Five-minute drive," Jorges said.

Pol cracked a grin and tried to remember what he had sounded like as a whining teenager. When he had the voice pegged, he reverted back to the slouched posture that had always gotten his father's goat and asked, "Gee, Dad, can I borrow the car...?"

Jorges laughed so hard he nearly dropped his shears.

PETE BANFIELD WAS GETTING the store ready for business, stocking shelves with freeze-dried fruit, trail rations and prepacked survival kits. It was a small shop in the heart of Reseda's business district, located between a Laundromat and a pawn shop and across the street from a club that alternated between holding rock concerts and wrestling matches. The secret of his success was a lean, well-monitored inventory and a willingness to serve the needs of his diverse clientele. Although a small section of the floor space was set aside for hard-core survivalists and other rugged individuals, most of his stock catered to suburbanites looking to halfheartedly prepare themselves for the chaos that would follow if the San Andreas Fault finally cut loose with the killer earthquake everyone had been predicting since the last big jolt fifteen years ago. All told, it was a thriving business for Pete. It was the first real success he'd had at anything since coming back from Vietnam with his body patched together with steel rods and molded plastic after a Cong booby-mine had chewed him up like something tossed into a Veg-o-matic. Miraculously, he still had the use of all his extremities, and provided he moved slowly, wore long sleeves and pants, kept taking his prescribed painkillers and meticulously avoided any discussion of his war experience, people would have a hard time believing that he had been left for dead on the battlefield. The severity of his wounds had convinced his fellow soldiers that they would have had more luck trying to put Humpty-Dumpty back together again.

He was at the cash register checking to see how much change he needed from the bank when a buzzer sounded back in the stockroom. Pete checked his watch. It was too early for freight deliveries. He quietly closed the register drawer and reached beneath the counter for a Soviet PPSh-41 subgun, the one illegal souvenir he'd brought back from Nam after taking it off the body of a Cong warrior whose plans of ambushing Banfield's outfit had come up short. It was something of a relic in terms of firearms, known more for its simplicity of design and low cost than for anything to do with its handling or performance. Still, it held thirty-five rounds of standard 7.62 mm bullets, and Pete figured that if things ever got bad enough that he needed some firepower, the PPSh-41 would do the job. Better to face the cops and try to explain his owning a burp gun than to end up pushing up daisies because he went up against somebody with more bullets than some sanctioned six-shooter.

The buzzer went off again as Pete tiptoed into the stockroom and made his way past the receiving desk and a stack of boxed potato flakes. Once he was next to the door, he stood off to one side and propped the subgun in firing position as he called out, "We aren't open yet. You'll have to come back later."

There was a pause on the other side of the door, then a reply.

"How unfortunate. I have a check from John Beresford Tipton made out to Pete Banfield for one million dollars. But if you're too busy..."

"Son of a bitch!" Pete shouted, lowering his gun and throwing open the dead bolt. It had to be the guy he'd bunked with during basic training. They'd gone through a nightly ritual of trying to outdo one another's plans regarding what they'd do if they had a chance to be the benefactor in the old TV series "The Millionaire." When he jerked the door open, Banfield saw Pol Blancanales standing in the alley, wearing one of his father's conservative suits and holding a piece of paper. The Politician kept a straight face, eyeing his old friend as if seeing him for the first time.

"You are Peter Banfield?"

"Yes," the shop owner intoned with mock gravity. "I am Peter Banfield."

"Then this is for you...."

Blancanales handed Pete the slip of paper. Banfield took one look at it and let loose with a yelp of laughter that sent him reeling backward into the doorframe. Instead of a check for a million dollars, Pol had given him an advertising for a free consultation with a plastic surgeon whose slogan was "Let us introduce you to the new you." In the margin, Pol had scrawled, "You qualify for our 50% off discount!"

Anyone else might have been taking his life in his hands by pulling such a prank on Banfield, but Blancanales wasn't just anyone. He and Pete traded high fives, then a longer, firmer handshake.

"Goddamn, is it good to see you," Pete said as he motioned for Blancanales to come into the shop. Eyeing Pol's graying hair, he quickly added, "Of course, I have to tell you up front that I don't stock Grecian Formula."

"Touché," Blancanales laughed.

"Come on in, have a look around."

Both men wandered into the front of the shop. Pol glanced over the stock and instinctively made his way to the hard-core survivalist offerings. "Nice," he said, scanning book titles on a wall rack. "Looks like you've got all the bases covered."

"I try. Hey, Blanc, what's with the limp?"

Pol waved away any need for concern. "Heavy metal mosquito bite. I don't scratch it for a few days and it'll go away."

"Yeah, right." Banfield started to put the Soviet automatic away, but Pol saw the gun and reached for it.

"Peter, Peter, this is a no-no."

"You ought to know all about that, hmmm?" Banfield let Blancanales have a closer look at the weapon.

"What's that supposed to mean?"

"I keep in touch with the guys," Pete said as he went back to checking the register. "Word gets around."

"And what's the word?"

Pete looked up from his petty cash, locking his gaze onto Blancanales. "Forget 'The Millionaire,' these days you're playing 'Mission: Impossible,' right?"

Blancanales sighed and handed the PPSh-41 back to Pete. "Ask me no questions, I'll tell you no lies," he replied, falling back on both men's favorite line during endless nights when they'd latched on to short-term dates to help them make the best of a three-day pass.

"Hell, I should've known you'd say that." Pete closed the register and paused to raid a pillbox for his morning dose of painkillers. Between swallows, he cracked, "And I bet if you ever get caught the secretary will disavow any knowledge of your actions."

Pol smiled, but there was a certain regret in the gesture. First Maria, then his father, and now Pete—all people close to him and yet left in the dark as to what his life was all about. All the secrecy bothered him, made him realize why he'd fallen out of touch with so many old friends and even with members of his own family. The Stony Man Curse, they called it back at headquarters. All the other men went through it in their own way, as well. Of course, Pol knew he could cut through the hush-hush to some extent if there was some reason to draw Pete into his confidence. Hell, Able Team had contacts all across the globe; people who could be plugged into any given assignment in a limited capacity and given at least some vague explanation as to what they were getting themselves into.

"That's it!" he muttered aloud as a metaphorical light bulb switched on in his mind.

"Say what?" Pete asked.

"Well, the way I see it," Pol reasoned, "if my orders are to kick back and relax until my leg gets better, then I guess that having a few drinks with an old buddy and getting a few things off my chest qualifies as a legitimate part of my assignment, don't you think?"

"I think I'm getting thirsty," Pete said. He checked the time, then motioned toward the back room. "I can't take booze with these pills I'm on, but I'll pretend if that's what it takes to loosen your tongue."

Shutting themselves off in Pete's office, the two men started working on a pot of freshly percolated coffee, and Pol gave his old bunk partner a sketching rundown on his role with the government's stateside terrorist-busters. He mentioned a few assignments, some of which Pete was vaguely familiar with, although the press versions of the same events had invariably painted a picture vastly different from what had actually happened.

"Naturally," Pol explained, "if we didn't cover our asses and the media caught wind of who we really were, there'd be a shitstorm of bad press that would make Watergate and the whole Irangate thing look like pranks at a birthday party."

"Well, I sure as hell ain't about to go hold a press conference, Blanc," Pete assured his ex-partner. He finished his coffee and noted with alarm that an hour had just slipped past them. "Christ, I gotta open shop!"

Pol accompanied Banfield into the store and gravitated back to the book rack as Pete went to open the front door.

"Hey, Blanc," Pete called out to him, "if you're really going stir-crazy and needed something to do, maybe you oughta check out that yellow card on the notice board."

The board held a wealth of business cards, promotional flyers, personal ads, sales blurbs and a few lost-and-found proclamations. The yellow card Pete had mentioned was in the upper right corner. It was a notice that an independent movie producer was looking for someone with an extensive paramilitary background to serve as creative consultant for a small budget feature film.

"Hmmm," Pol droned. "Sounds intriguing. What the hell's a 'creative consultant'?"

"Kinda like a technical advisor," Pete told him. "I did a stint like that for a film a couple years back. You sit around and tell the producer and director and actors the way things would really be done, then they ignore everything you tell them and do things their way and wonder why the movie bombs at the box office."

"Had a lot of fun, did you?"

"Easiest money I ever made legally," Banfield boasted. "And the ladies on the set—how does that song go?—they love a man in a uniform."

"You know anything about this producer?"

Pete shook his head. "Just got posted yesterday. My day off. If you're interested, you better go for it while the iron's still hot."

"I guess it wouldn't hurt to check this out." Blancanales pried the yellow notice from the board and slipped it into his pocket. A few customers had already filtered into the shop, and Pol waved to Pete on his way out the door.

"Hollywood, here I come," he declared confidently.

"I just hope they're ready for you," Pete called after him.

2

Carl Lyons crouched his one-hundred-and-ninety-pound frame over the newly laid railroad tracks, focusing his attention on a strange contraption straddling the rails. It was a small flatbed car, roughly the size of a Red Rider wagon he remembered playing with during his youth in Pasadena. The wheels were reinforced by swing-down mounts to keep the vehicle from being jarred off the tracks, and rising up lengthwise from the bed was a thick single sheet of space-laminate armored plating that looked vaguely like a bulky, petrified sail. Although there was a frigid wind blowing across this isolated pocket of Virginia's Shenandoah Valley, the sheet provided no sailing function. Instead, the rail car was propelled by a small modified Briggs & Stratton engine that had in a former life worked the blades of a power mower.

Keeping his gloves on, Lyons primed the engine's small carburetor, then closed his fingers around the starter handle. "Okay, baby, talk to me," he whispered, then jerked hard on the starting cord. The engine sputtered uncertainly and died. Lyons readjusted the manual choke and tried again. This time the engine caught and spit a cloud of exhaust as it roared to life. Lyons eased up on the choke, then engaged the clutch and stepped back as the four-wheeled oddity began rolling down the tracks in a herky-jerky motion, always varying its speed.

"Okay, Cowboy," Lyons murmured under his breath, "take 'er away...."

Cowboy Kissinger and Gadgets Schwarz were a hundred yards away, hidden from Lyons's view by a cluster of boulders. The moment they heard the mating cry of the Briggs & Stratton, they scrambled down from the rocks and bee-lined for a pair of wooden crates with the same dimensions as coffins. In one of the crates was a stock Barrett Light .50 Model 82 rifle, thirty-five pounds and sixty-six inches of armor-penetrating semiautomatic firepower. The other crate contained Kissinger's most recently modified version of the same weapon, which was six pounds lighter and seven inches shorter. Cowboy grabbed the latter rifle while Gadgets stuck to the standard model. Both men quickly backtracked to the boulder formation and readied their guns, using bipods for stability and ten-power scopes to draw beads on their target, the sporadically moving target vehicle on the distant stretch of rails. The lightness and shortened length of Kissinger's rifle gave him a few seconds lead in setting up. Both men were gifted marksmen, and once they had sighted their target they drowned out the Briggs & Stratton with peals of gunfire, blasting .50 caliber rounds at the upright sheet of armor plating.

Normally, the Barrett's ammunition consisted of Browning Machine Gun cartridges with 750-grain projectiles that far outweighed anything a smaller gun might have to offer. However, Kissinger had doctored the bullets with dyes—red for his shots, blue for Gadgets's—so that they would be able to tell whose shots had struck home with the greatest accuracy. As the rolling target took a series of direct hits and all but jumped off the tracks from the collective impact, it became pocked with more reds and blues than the American flag.

Reaching the end of its run, the target cart rolled over a trip-wire that disconnected its spark plug, shutting down the engine. The same swing-down mounts that had kept the car on the rails now served as brakes and brought the vehicle to a stop, less than a dozen yards from the shoveled tarmac that served as an airstrip for Stony Man Farm.

"So what do you think?" Kissinger asked Schwarz as the two men left the rock formation and began walking across the snow-covered ground toward the airstrip.

"We'll have to check the targets to make sure," Gadgets said, cradling the standard Barrett in his hands, "but I'm pretty sure you won."

The whole purpose of the exercise was to make certain the modifications to the Barrett didn't sacrifice reliability for portability, and when they reached the stilled target and saw that Kissinger's red marks slightly outnumbered Schwarz's blues, both men grunted with satisfaction. There was also little difference in the extent of penetration by the bullets, a major concern of Cowboy's when he had shortened the M-82's barrel.

"Looks like you got the bugs out this time, Cowboy," Lyons said as he joined them. He packed a snowball in his hands and tossed it at the target, hitting a bull's-eye. "Hell, if we can get these Barretts into action a few seconds quicker without losing accuracy, there's gonna be a lot more low-lifes getting their butts nailed before they can make get-aways."

"Yeah, well, that's the whole idea, isn't it?" Kissinger commented, beaming with the satisfaction he always felt when he took a good weapon and found a way to make it better.

A telltale drone turned the men's heads eastward. Above the forested peaks of the Blue Ridge Mountains they could see a growing speck in the leaden sky. The speck eventually took the shape of a twin-engine C-12 utility plane. Given to the Stony Man operation out of Army inventory, the plane had been repainted and stenciled with the name of a nonexistent courier service. It was just one of several aircraft used by operatives on their never-ending range of assignments. In this case, the plane was on its way back from Washington, where Stony Man's head of operations, Hal Brognola, had spent the past two days in meetings with the attorney general and a few ranking members of the Justice Department.

When he stepped out of the plane, looking haggard and irritable, the welcoming committee on the ground had the distinct feeling that their boss had not returned with pleasant tidings....

"HIS NAME'S NASH FELSUR."

Brognola passed a photo of the man to Lyons. They were in the conference room at headquarters, gathered around the fabled table where so many hard decisions had been made over the years. Kissinger sat next to Lyons, and across from them were Schwarz and Lao Ti, the deceptively petite research aide who had returned to the Farm with Brognola after an extended leave of absence to care for her ailing parents back in Taiwan. Jack Grimaldi, the wisecracking fly-boy who had been at the controls of the C-12, was at the end of the table opposite Brognola.

"Nash Felsur?" Grimaldi repeated the name. "Sounds like the name of a car that came out around the time of the Edsel."

"I was hoping that with Blancanales on sick leave I might finally be able to hold a briefing without one-liners," Brognola snapped. The sour mood he'd left Washington with still hadn't mellowed. He'd started out the meeting clutching one of his ever-present prop cigars, but in his state he'd inadvertently snapped it in half and hadn't bothered to unwrap a replacement.

"Sorry, chief," Grimaldi apologized.

Gadgets took the photo of Felsur from Lyons and looked over the pallid, frail features of an obviously ill man who had shrunk to the point where his tailored suit hung loosely on him. He had horn-rimmed glasses with thick lenses that made his eyes look as oversized as his suit.

"Mob?" he guessed.

Brognola nodded. "He's based out of Cincinnati, but he's had his meat hooks in the action throughout the Midwest for years. Has ties with the big families in Chicago, Detroit, Cleveland...hell, just about everywhere between here and Vegas."

"And we're supposed to track him down and put him out of his misery, right?" Lyons speculated, relishing the thought.

"No," Brognola replied tersely. "We're supposed to protect him."

"What?" Schwarz and Lyons blurted simultaneously.

"You heard me."

"Christ, chief," Lyons went on, "I knew you didn't look well when you got off the plane, but with all due respect, did those geeks at Justice slip something in your drink when you weren't looking?"

Brognola eyed the Ironman warningly. "Who do you think you're talking to?"

"I don't know; some Mafia stooge dolled up to look like Hal Brognola, from the sounds of it." A flush of red was creeping up past Lyons's collar, and anger blazed in his ice-blue eyes.

"Let me explain...."

"Have you run this one past Mack Bolan yet?" Lyons cut in, referring to the man behind the initial conception of the Stony Man operation. He slammed his fist on the table for emphasis. "Hell, no, and I can sure as shit imagine why. Bolan spent years butting his head against the mob, and you know damn well what his guidelines were. No quarter, no mercy, no deals. And now you're telling us we're supposed to *protect* one of these scumbags?''

In the wake of Lyons's outburst there was a moment's silence. Brognola took advantage of the lull to regain his own composure. He went through his coat pockets for a cigar and idly rolled it between his fingers, if only to demonstrate to the others that he was in control again.

''Are you finished, Carl?'' he asked Lyons calmly. ''Or did someone put you in charge of this organization while I was away?''

It wasn't like Brognola to be sarcastic, and the retort served to put Lyons back in his place.

''Okay, okay, so I shot my mouth off before I had all the facts,'' he grumbled. ''I just don't cotton much to coddling anyone in the mob, period.''

''Point made and point taken,'' Brognola said. Indicating the others, he added, ''And I'm sure that we all are of a same mind. But I have to point out to you that although I may run things around here, my orders still come from Washington, and when they say jump we go airborne.

''Now, as far as Felsur goes, the story's this . . . the guy's got cancer crawling through him faster than doctors can get it out, and he's decided he wants to put a few things in order before his time's up.''

''Confession?'' Schwarz said.

''Yes, and not to a priest, either,'' Brognola resumed. ''He wants to go before a grand jury. The man knows names, places . . . where bodies are buried. He can do the mob a world of hurt.''

''And they're sure as hell going to try to do him a world of hurt before he sings,'' Grimaldi said. ''That's where we come in, right?''

By way of reply, Brognola passed around blowup maps of Cincinnati and environs. ''Right now he's knee-deep in U.S. Marshals in a private cell, but part of the deal he cut with the

D.A. was that he could be with his wife somewhere away from bars until he goes into a witness relocation program after his testimony.

"Tomorrow they're moving him out to this country estate." He pointed out a dot on the map north of the city, near the Hamilton County Fair Grounds. "Since we figure there might be a hit right off, most of the marshals will be escorting a decoy somewhere else. Felsur goes out later with a less conspicuous bodyguard."

"Us," Lyons ventured.

"You and Schwarz will be at his side," Brognola told the Able Team principals. "Lao Ti and Grimaldi will go along to handle the peripheries. You'll all leave after supper."

"I think I lost my appetite," Lyons muttered.

As the group filed out of the conference room, Lao Ti spoke for the first time since the meeting had started. "I guess Pol picked a good time to be out of action, yes?"

"There's the understatement of the decade," Grimaldi said. "I wonder what the hell he's up to out in California, anyway?"

3

Blancanales opted for the scenic route to Hollywood, getting off the San Diego Freeway at Sunset Boulevard and heading east. To his right was UCLA, alive with the bustling activity of students who seemed to be getting younger every year. He still found it hard to believe that his baby sister was the same age as the coeds he saw jogging along the campus perimeter.

Across from the university was Bel Air, with lavish, cloistered estates that easily rivaled the high-priced Beverly Hills digs farther down the road. The entire area reeked of wealth and prestige: from the Jaguars and Mercedeses prowling Sunset to the Rollses and Bentleys parked in horseshoe driveways; from the manicured lawns and luxurious flower beds to the neocolonial mansions and other sprawling architectural wonders where nannies and servants only barely outnumbered the groundskeepers and gardeners who flitted about the estates like drone bees, keeping up appearances.

Blancanales felt uncomfortable in the presence of so much conspicuous wealth, and not only because he was driving his father's '78 Chevy. All his life he'd known the brutal gap that existed between the haves and the have-nots, and as an entrenched member of the latter group he'd always resented the rich. It wasn't so much the money they had or the things they bought. It had more to do with the way they paraded themselves around as people of privilege. He remembered when he'd been a busboy at his parents' restaurant, and how the wealthier patrons had invariably been the ones who talked down to him the most, who treated him as if he was no more than some disposable possession that came with the meal. And he could recall the conversations that he'd heard while he was busing tables, all the petty whining and bitching about insignificant problems, spoiled housewives acting as if having to switch interior decorators was a major calamity. None of their complaints came close to the sort of dilemmas Pol was faced with, like whether he was going to be beat up by gang members on the way to school or if his folks would make enough money that month that he could finally go to the dentist to have a tooth pulled that was so painful that some nights he went to bed crying. He'd seen a lot of the world since those days in East L.A. and San Ysidro, but no matter where he was, be it Vietnam, Nicaragua, Louisiana or the nation's capital, there always seemed to be the same universal struggle going on, and his instincts invariably made him side with the underdog.

Coming out of Beverly Hills and into the high-rise heaven of West Hollywood, Blancanales was tempted to forget about his appointment with the film producer. What did he think he was trying to prove, anyway? That he could sell out as easily as the next guy when the right opportunity knocked?

Waiting at a traffic light, Blancanales idly glanced off to his right where patio diners were having lunch under Cinzano umbrellas at a posh restaurant. It was apparently someone's birthday, because a pair of women dressed as walking cakes began singing in front of one of the tables, seductively removing "slices" from their costumes at the end of each verse. The recipient of the striptease was blushing while the others at the table cheered the cake ladies on. Everyone else joined in the celebration, and by the time the traffic light had changed, the two girls had stripped down to pasties and G-strings in the shapes of valentine hearts. They received applause for their efforts, and Pol couldn't help but grin at the sight.

Enough with the social commentary, Blancanales, he chided himself as he drove on. Lighten up and enjoy yourself, why don't you? That's what vacations are for. Live a little. Stop and smell the roses and all that other good shit, eh?

"Yeah, why not?" he whispered aloud. He noticed that the man in the car beside him had one arm out the window and was drumming his fingers on the roof in time with the music blaring from his radio. "Yeah, why not?" Pol told himself again as he cranked up his own receiver and tuned in to a local oldies station, filling the Chevy with the carefree strains of the Beach Boys.

He sang along, shaking off the last of his doldrums and checking street addresses until he located the building where his appointment was scheduled. Hell, this should be a lark, he decided. His chance to hobnob and dabble with Hollywood, and face it, what red-blooded American boy raised on John Wayne and Paul Newman movies didn't harbor a secret urge to check out what things were like on the other side of that silver screen?

Pol wasn't able to find a parking spot on the street, so he reluctantly headed into the underground garage located beneath the Cal-Loan office building. With even greater reluctance he surrendered his father's car keys to a young Hispanic valet in a burgundy blazer. Blancanales had parked cars for a few months as a teenager, and he knew the sort of abuse a vehicle could be put through during the short time it took to get from the drop-off point to a parking spot beyond the owner's view. Tipping the valet two dollars in advance, Blancanales cheerfully advised the youth in Spanish not to do anything to the car that he didn't want done to himself.

"Si, amigo," the valet said with a wink. "Don't worry, I only go joyriding in the BMWs."

Blancanales took an elevator up to the eighth floor, then walked down a spotless corridor to the last door on the right. A placard on the door read: YouRan Productions. Pol took a deep breath, then let himself in.

A pert brunette receptionist glanced up from her copy of *Daily Variety* and offered a practiced smile. "Good afternoon. Are you the Mr. Blancanales who called earlier today?"

"Uh, yes." Pol eyeballed the waiting room. It was sparsely but expensively furnished: overstuffed chairs, potted palms, prints on walls painted the color of money. The plush carpet made him feel as if he was walking on clouds.

The woman rose from behind her desk as she continued to smile. Blancanales wondered if her face was stuck that way. "And you brought your résumé?" she asked.

Pol nodded and reached into his pocket for the paper she'd requested over the phone. He'd typed it up at his folks' place before lunch, listing his military service and giving fleeting mention to a few other endeavors he could claim credit for without jeopardizing the security of his position with Able Team.

The secretary took the résumé in exchange for a stapled film treatment. As Blancanales glanced over the document, the secretary explained, "If you could just take a seat and look this over, Mr. Bendellan will be with you shortly."

The woman headed off into a back office. Blancanales plopped into one of the chairs and began flipping through the treatment. The film's working title was *You Ran, Iran* and the basic story line concerned a group of Delta Force commandos who successfully reclaim a cache of stolen explosives from Iranian terrorists. At first glance, the story line struck Pol as being as ridiculous as the title, but he quickly acknowledged that he was here for a job as technical adviser and not as screenwriter. When Pol had called Pete Banfield before leaving for Hollywood, the vet's biggest piece of advice had been, "Whatever you do, don't take things too seriously, and remember that you'll probably be dealing with flakes who spend half their income letting shrinks, accountants and palm readers do their thinking for them."

A lark, Pol reminded himself.

The secretary returned, smile still planted on her face. "Mr. Bendellan will see you now. He's our associate producer."

Pol followed her into a side office that offered a view of the Hollywood Hills, with their legendary sign and the glowing dome of Griffith Observatory. Sitting behind a mahogany desk that took up nearly half the room was a lean blond man in a charcoal-brown suit. He was on the phone, but quickly hung up and extended a hand to Blancanales. "Hi, I'm Otto Bendellan," he introduced himself with a smooth, measured voice.

"Rosario Blancanales," Pol said, shaking the other man's hand, noting the variety of rings cluttering his fingers. "Pleased to meet you."

"Likewise. Have a seat."

Blancanales chose a chair opposite from Bendellan's desk. As he expected, the seat was set low so that he was forced to look up at the man interviewing him. Bendellan looked to be in his early forties, with pale gray eyes and a salon tan. He fingered a trim mustache below his broad nose as he glanced over Blancanales's résumé.

"Very impressive, Mr. Blancanales. Done a lot of mercenary work since your Army days, is that it?"

"Something like that," Pol answered evasively.

"And you had a chance to look over the treatment?"

Pol nodded. "Lotta action scenes, from the looks of it."

"Precisely." Bendellan leaned back in his chair, picking up a quarter and idly rolling it across his fingers like a magician in spring training. "Why don't we talk about some of those scenes for a minute?"

"So you can test me and make sure I'm legit?" Pol surmised.

"That, and to get a feel for your specific areas of expertise." Bendellan shifted the coin to his other hand. "How about if we jump ahead and start with the climactic scene. Given what's in the treatment, how would you block out the raid? The more technical the better. Of course, it might do to keep in mind we're not Spielberg, so you'll have to be realistic in terms of our budget."

Tactical strategy was usually the province of Carl Lyons, and finding himself in the position of calling the shots was a rare treat for Pol, something he hadn't even considered when applying for the consulting job. All of a sudden this was more than a lark again. It was a challenge, and he rose to the occasion. While Bendellan nodded his head and scribbled notes, Pol launched into an ad-lib planning session, building on the information in the film treatment and making sure he threw in as much technical jargon as possible. He proposed alternatives for every stage of the operation—explaining how Ingrams compared with Uzis as submachine guns, when it might be advantageous to use M-16s rather than M-10s, the benefits of predawn assaults—all the while improvising and drawing upon his years of experience in the type of undertaking YouRan Productions proposed dramatizing. Inspired, Blancanales left his seat several times, pointing to imaginary sentries or blocking out scenarios on Bendellan's desk, using paperweights and pens for props.

More than a half hour had passed before Pol finished his spiel and sat back in the chair, letting the adrenaline bottom out inside him. Noticing the time, he grinned sheepishly at Bendellan. "I guess maybe I got a little carried away, but you get the general idea."

"I certainly do," Bendellan replied, "and I'm impressed, I have to say. I'm expecting the finished script this afternoon, and, of course, anything you do would have to coincide with that."

"Of course," Pol said.

"We figure you'd be on the job for two weeks, and we'll be doing most of the shooting in Indiana, just outside Indianapolis. We'd probably be out there by the end of the week. Any problem with any of that?"

"Not that I can see."

"Good, good. Well, then, Mr. Blancanales. The job is yours if you want it."

Blancanales did his best to keep a straight face. He expected that there were probably dozens of people to be interviewed and that it would be at least a few days before he knew if he'd passed the first hurdle. Bendellan's offer took him totally by surprise.

"There's still a few details we haven't discussed," he managed to sputter.

"Of course." Bendellan reached into one of his desk drawers for a document, which he handed to Pol. "This is a standard work-for-hire agreement. Have a look, and we'll fill in your name and get it processed pronto."

Blancanales's poker face nearly crumbled when he looked at the base pay he'd be receiving for two weeks of work. The Army hadn't paid him that much the whole time he was in Nam. And there was an expense account on top of that to provide for meals and lodging and God knows what else they expected him to buy with so much petty cash. Hell, and he was so jazzed about playing sidelines general that he'd been thinking about taking on the job for free! This was too much.

Or was it?

Pol remembered another piece of advice Pete had given him. "Don't play too easy to get, or those bastards won't respect you. Drive the hardest damn bargain you can swing, and be ready to walk away from it or you won't get anywhere."

Blancanales made a face and set the slip of paper back on Bendellan's desk, then leaned back in his chair and yawned as he glanced out the window, pretending to admire the scenery.

"Is there some problem?" the man in the suit inquired.

"Well, Otto, this strikes me as a fairly reasonable offer," Pol drawled lazily, enjoying the charade. He'd already plotted his way of playing hardball with the man on the other side of the deck. "But," he continued, "well, how can I put it? I have this kid sister who's been trying to get her acting career off the ground. Nothing big, you understand. Just something to get her feet wet, so to speak. And I noticed in that treatment that there's a few parts that might be right up her alley...."

"I see." Bendellan smiled thinly, then rose from his seat. "Casting isn't my department, but if you'll excuse me a minute I might be able to come up with something, okay?"

Pol put his hands behind his head and swung his feet up onto the coffee table. "No hurry," he told Bendellan. "I'll just catch up on the trades...."

While Bendellan stepped out of the office, Blancanales picked up a copy of the *Hollywood Reporter* and smirked to himself as he read the latest industry news. Shit, if only Lyons and Schwarz could see him now, he thought. Poor bastards would turn a serious shade of green. Even if he'd bargained himself out of the job, Pol figured that the interview was already worth a few good stories once he got back to Stony Man Farm.

He was perusing the list of the week's top box-office hits when Bendellan reappeared with a tall, svelte woman with auburn hair and deep green eyes.

"I think we can accommodate both you and your sister, Mr. Blancanales," the woman said, smiling brightly as Pol rose to meet her.

"You're the producer, then?" Pol asked, taken aback by the woman's stunning beauty.

"That's right," she replied. "My name's Mae Jung."

"Glad to meet you, Ms. Jung." Pol shook the woman's hand. There was some interesting chemistry between them. He found himself wondering if maybe they might end up getting together for an experiment.

"Please," the woman insisted, "call me Mae."

She would have been more accurate if she'd asked him to call her Claudette Simms.

4

Jorges Blancanales was running a gas-powered edger along his sidewalk when he first spied the white stretch limousine turning onto his street. It was an uncommon enough sight in this part of town that the elderly man kept his eye on the vehicle and stalled out his edger when the whirring steel blades wandered off course and bit into the unyielding concrete with a shower of sparks. Cursing himself for being distracted and venting an equal torrent of profanity on the limo, Jorges crouched over the edger to inspect the blades. They were nicked but still serviceable.

To Jorges's surprise, the limousine slowed to a stop alongside the curb in front of him. The car's windows were tinted, blocking his view of those inside. However, the driver's door soon opened and a man wearing a chauffeur's uniform emerged, circling stiffly around the front of the vehicle and nodding a terse greeting to the elder Blancanales.

"What are you doing here?" Jorges demanded.

By way of reply, the chauffeur opened the back passenger door and Pol Blancanales climbed out, still wearing his father's suit along with a few additional Hollywood touches. Instead of a white shirt, he wore a Hawaiian print with an open collar, exposing several layers of fake gold chains, and his eyes were hidden behind a pair of mirror-surfaced sunglasses.

At first Jorges didn't recognize his son. When he did, he wished he hadn't. *"Madre de Dios,"* he murmured, shaking his head with disapproval. "My son looks like a pimp!"

Pol lowered his glasses enough so that Jorges could see him wink. "Just having some fun, Pops, that's all."

"Where is my Chevy?"

"It's at the rental place where I got this."

"My Chevy's not good enough for you?"

"Come on, Pops, relax." Pol saw his sister bursting out of the house and quickly propped the sunglasses back up on his nose. "This is for Pixie, okay?" he told Jorges.

The older man snorted his disapproval and went back to his edger as Maria crossed the lawn to her brother's side. Close behind her was another girl of college age, light-skinned with beguiling hazel eyes. Both of the girls were carrying books.

"Would you look at that!" Maria marveled, her eyes on the limousine. "You aren't going to tell me you traded in Dad's car...."

Pol shook his head, putting on his best mogul's grin. "Actually, sweetheart, I'm gonna make you a star and I figured I'd take you to the top in style."

"What?" Maria looked at her brother worriedly. "Rosie, did you spend too much time on the beach or what?"

"I'll tell you about it on the way to dinner."

Pol gestured to Pete Banfield, who was playing chauffeur. Pete reopened the door and held it while Pol gestured for the girls to get in.

"Rosie, this is Veronica Rammite," Maria said. "We're taking the same drama class at Pierce. Veronica, this is my brother, Rosario."

"An honor, my dear," Pol said, taking the young woman's hand and bowing slightly as he kissed it.

Veronica blushed as she got into the car. "Maria never told me she had a brother in the film business."

"It's news to me, too, Ronnie," Maria told her friend.

Pol exchanged glances with his father before getting into the limo. Jorges had a sour look on his face. He shook his head and turned away from his son, starting up the edger so that it would drown out the sound of the limo. Pol sighed and got in the front seat. It was too bad the old man didn't have a sense of humor, he thought, but he wasn't going to let that spoil his fun. As Pete headed off, Pol explained the arrangement he'd made with YouRan Productions and told Maria about her bit part in *You Ran, Iran*.

"You're kidding!" Maria shrieked excitedly. "I don't believe it!"

"Well, it's true, so you'd better get used to it," Pol replied. "Right now, we're going to celebrate. I already got paid a little up front."

"So I guessed," Maria said, running her fingers over the leather armrests of the limousine. "This is a long way from *La Cucaracha*. Say, Rosie, do you think you could get them to find a part for Veronica?"

"No, that's okay," Veronica insisted.

Looking at her in the rearview mirror, Pol could see the hungry, hopeful look in the young woman's eyes.

"I'll see what I can do," he promised.

A few blocks later, Pete pulled into the parking lot of a modest-looking Mexican restaurant at the edge of the barrio. He had recommended the place to Pol as one of the best eateries in this part of the Valley. As he got out of the car and prepared to open the back door for the girls, he suddenly stopped.

A gang of five youths in their late teens appeared from out of a back alley that ran behind the restaurant. Wearing sleeveless T-shirts, jeans and sneakers, they nonchalantly fanned out to circle the limousine. There was no one else in the parking lot, which was partially shielded from the street by a large hedge and an even larger billboard.

The leader of the gang ran his fingers through his slicked-back hair and whistled softly as he eyed the vehicle. When his gaze drifted up and met with Banfield's, he grinned maliciously. *"Buenos dias."*

"Si," Pete agreed calmly, taking a step away from the limo. "And it'll go on being a nice day if you guys keep walking...."

The gang leader shrugged. "Why walk when we can drive?"

Inside the limo, Pol quickly sized up the situation and told the women in the back seat to stay put. As he started to get out, Maria reached for his arm. "Your leg—"

"Don't worry," Pol assured her. "I won't drop-kick anyone unless I have to."

"Be careful...."

By the time Pol was out of the limo, hell was already breaking loose in the parking lot. Three youths were making their move on Pete, and the other two were pulling out switchblades as they approached the passenger doors from opposite sides of the vehicle.

Blancanales was able to quickly reduce the odds by ducking the blade of his closest opponent and countering with a sharp karate jab to the shorter youth's midsection, knocking the wind from his lungs so that he doubled over, gasping for breath. A follow-up chop to the neck flattened him across the pavement.

Injured though he was, Blancanales was still in good enough shape to spring off his good leg and, using one arm as a pivot, vault over the hood of the limo and into two of the thugs trying to overpower Pete. Pol took the two men down, ignoring a jolt of pain that shot through his leg when he landed. He rendered a flurry of close-quarters bo jitsu moves that quickly immobilized his opponents before they could make use of their chains.

Pete gave a good account of himself, yanking off his chauffeur's cap and flinging it into the face of the gang leader. He took advantage of the teen's distraction by delivering one of the fierce right uppercuts that had made him the top-ranked middleweight in basic training. The other man's teeth slammed shut as his jaw took the blow, and he staggered backward into the only other gang member still on his feet.

The final opponent shoved his leather aside and moved away from the limousine, lashing out with his switchblade. His quickness took Banfield by surprise, and Pete was unable to avoid the gleaming edge of steel that bit sharply through the upper left sleeve of his chauffeur's jacket. To the hood's astonishment, however, he wasn't able to pull the blade free. Before he was able to let go of the weapon, Pete pulled his arm inward, dragging his stunned foe within range of his potent fist. A right cross sent the Hispanic youth toppling onto his leader, who was still groping for his senses on the pavement.

It hadn't taken Pete and Pol more than fifteen seconds to neutralize the gang, and when the owner of the restaurant came bursting out the kitchen door, toting a shotgun, the youths abandoned any thoughts of a second assault. Though battered and bruised, none of the gang members were seriously injured, and they staggered off into the dusk as both the owner and Blancanales shouted warnings for them to stay clear of the restaurant if they knew what was good for them.

The owner, a stocky, balding man with a thick silver mustache, apologized for the altercation and asked the men if they were okay.

"I'm fine," Pol said, testing his sore leg with a few steps toward Banfield. "How about you, Pete? They caught you with a good one, didn't they?"

"Sort of." Banfield tugged hard, jerking the switchblade from his arm as Pol watched in stunned silence. Pete chuckled slightly and tapped the arm with the blade's handle, giving off a slightly hollow sound. "The miracles of modern plastic," he joked, giving Pol a glimpse of the partial prosthesis that held his left arm together beneath the slit fabric of his coat.

The owner promised them free drinks with dinner, then headed back into the kitchen. Behind Pol and Banfield, Maria and Veronica emerged from the limousine, both ashen from what they had witnessed.

"Tell you what," Pete told the others. "Now that we've had our fun, how about if you guys go eat and I'll take this tank back while it's still in one piece. I think maybe the Chevy will be a little less conspicuous."

"Might be a good idea," Pol said. He offered the girls a comforting grin. "Well, everybody always says that film stars lead exciting lives, right? Come on, let's get inside and have something to eat."

"Just order me a burrito to go," Pete said as he got back inside the limousine and started the engine.

As the others headed for the restaurant, Maria glanced warily at the alley where the gang had disappeared. "What if they come back?"

"I don't think we have to worry about that," Pol said. "I grew up around my share of gangs, remember? My guess is they'll be licking their wounds for a few more hours before they go prowling again, and I don't think they'll come back here knowing they could end up with their butts full of buckshot."

"I hope you're right," Maria said.

"Hey, come on," Pol said, putting his arms around both girls' shoulders. "This is supposed to be a celebration. Let's see some smiles here!"

ACROSS THE STREET from the restaurant, Otto Bendellan lowered his binoculars and started up the Buick Regal he'd parked along the curb. He rounded the corner and traveled two blocks to a side alley separating a supermarket from a run-down housing complex. The five gang members who had caused the disturbance at the parking lot were waiting for him near a trash dumpster, cursing the blows they'd taken. He'd already given each youth an advance of twenty dollars, and as he put the Regal in neutral and rolled down his window he peeled another five twenties from his money clip before slipping it back inside his coat pocket.

"Nice job, boys," he told them.

The gang leader took the money, then grabbed Bendellan's wrist and came out with his switchblade, placing the edge against the thin layer of flesh above the man's veins.

"Mas," he demanded.

"More?" Bendellan calmly said. "This is what we agreed on."

"Mas!"

"Okay, okay!" Bendellan reached inside his coat, knowing that the leader had seen him put the money clip there. What the leader didn't know was that, along with the clip, Bendellan's coat held another means of persuasion. With a fluid motion, the associate producer yanked out a Colt Cobra Model D-3 and gave the gang leader a guided tour of its 102 mm barrel. The lightweight revolver held six 200-grain slugs capable of doing what they did best at a muzzle velocity of 223 meters per second.

"Get that fucking knife outta my arm and take a hike or I'm gonna pick your nose so there's nothing left of it."

The gang leader slowly pulled his switchblade away from Bendellan's wrist. When Otto pulled back the hammer, all five of the youths collectively ran off, slipping through a gap in the fence that led to the housing project.

Bendellan kept the gun in his lap as he pulled out of the alley and onto one of the main roads leading back to the freeway. On the way, he grabbed the cellular phone mounted between the two front seats and placed a call. He got an answer on the fifth ring.

"Yes?" It was Claudette Simms.

"I just checked him out in action," Bendellan reported. "Guy knows how to handle himself, all right."

"Good," Claudette responded. "I did a check on his record, and most of his résumé checked out. There are a lot of gaps unaccounted for, and I've got a feeling there's probably some mercenary work he doesn't want to own up to."

"That'll work in our favor," Bendellan said.

"Precisely," Claudette said. "I think that our Mr. Blancanales is going to make a perfect fall guy...."

5

"They didn't go for the bait," U.S. Marshal Abe Abko told Gadgets Schwarz and Carl Lyons.

"Is that good or bad?" Schwarz wondered, already suspecting the answer.

"I guess you could call it either way," Abko said. "However, my money says it ain't good."

They were in an antechamber at the Hamilton County Jail just outside Cincinnati. Nash Felsur was still in custody down the hall, conversing with his lawyer.

Lyons's distaste for the assignment hadn't abated any over the past twelve hours. "This whole damn thing was done ass-backwards if you ask me," he complained, rising from his chair and starting to pace the hard floor.

"Not that anyone *did* ask you," Abko drawled, "but what would you have done differently?"

"If you're going to have a decoy transfer, you should do it simultaneous with the real thing," Lyons ventured. "That way you don't end up back at square one if the decoy plan doesn't pan out."

Abko was a burly man with thick skin when it came to taking advice from outsiders, especially when they blew into town with a lot of advance notice about how they were supposed to receive preferential treatment because they were "specialists." He cracked his knuckles methodically as he leaned against the wall, wishing he could break Lyons's bones just as easily. "That's your opinion now, isn't it?"

"Yeah, and now it's our problem, too," Lyons growled. In a way he could sympathize with the marshal's attitude toward him, but he wasn't in the mood for working at public relations. Their already lousy assignment had just taken a turn for the worse.

Schwarz put it into words. "Well, Marshal, if your intelligence people caught wind that the mob was going to come after Felsur and then they didn't even sniff at the decoy, we've got two likely options. Either your people were mistaken or else the mob knew that the decoy was just that, in which case they know how the real transfer's supposed to go down."

"You, too?" Abko said. "Man, this is great. Stereo bitching."

The verbal sparring seemed destined to escalate further when a door down the hallway opened and Nash Felsur stepped into view alongside his attorney. Felsur looked frailer than in his photograph, and each step he took looked as if it could be his last. The attorney, on the other hand, strode with robust determination, leaving the mobster to catch up to him as he joined the others. Clovis Bronson was a man used to having his way.

"I hope everything's in order, Marshal," he told Abko.

"I don't think we should move him until we rethink things," Lyons interjected.

"And why not?" There was an imperious tone in the lawyer's deep, booming voice. "I was under the impression that this had all been worked out."

"It has," Abko insisted, stepping forward and trying to wedge himself between the lawyer and the two men from Able Team.

"Don't get me wrong," Lyons said, eyeing the lawyer with the same insolence he'd used on Abko. "If your boy gets his ass shot off like a sitting duck, I won't lose any sleep over it . . . except that my ass would apt to be in the shooting gallery along with him, and that just doesn't sit well with me, *capiche*?''

"I want to be with my wife," Nash Felsur declared as he finally made his way to his lawyer's side. Although his voice was weak, it was still filled with resolution. "Now!" he snapped.

"Easy, Nash," Bronson told his client. "No need to get riled. There's no way the D.A. will stand for you getting the runaround this close to your hearing. Right, Marshal?"

"That's the way I see it, Mr. Bronson," Abko said. "Of course, these gentlemen are calling the shots on this one, so we're at their mercy."

"I see." Bronson raised one arm and pulled back on the sleeve of his suit to reveal a gold-encrusted watch. He checked the time, then looked at Lyons. "If my client isn't on the way to his safehouse in five minutes, I call the D.A."

Lyons knew that if the D.A. raised a stink and word got back to Washington, he'd be getting a dose of Brognola-style fire and brimstone soon after. Not an appealing thought.

"Fine, we'll play it your way," Lyons said, giving in.

He excused himself and signaled for Gadgets to follow him. They walked around the corner to an isolated niche out of the other men's earshot.

"Real batch of Einsteins we're dealing with here, eh, Ironman?"

"Tell me about it."

Lyons unclipped a palm-sized communicator from his belt. Aaron Kurtzman and Lao Ti had collaborated in the creation of the device back at Stony Man Farm. In essence, it was a cross between a conventional walkie-talkie and the space-age contraptions used by the crew of the U.S.S. Enterprise on *Star Trek*. Lao Ti considered herself a consummate Trekkie, and the communicator was only one of that show's inventions that she had spent considerable time trying to duplicate in a twentieth-century setting. Lyons honed in on a prearranged frequency to make contact with Lao Ti.

"We've checked all the roads on the scheduled route," the Oriental woman reported. "Everything seems clear, but there's just too many potential ambush sites. Grimaldi says you'd be better off using the highways, and I have to agree with him."

"Makes sense the way things have been going," Lyons concurred. As he brought her up to date on the situation at the jail, he pulled out a local map and started improvising a new strategy. "Okay, this is the way we'll run it. Instead of taking the route we're supposed to, we'll hop on the 275 and swing all the way around to where it links up with the 75, then we'll head back down and get off at Hamstead."

"Okay," came the reply over the small speaker on Lyons's communicator. "What do you want us to do?"

"Why don't you cover the exit ramp at Hamstead and have Grimaldi post up near the safehouse. I'll make sure to have the locals fall back as reinforcements. Hopefully that will shake things up enough to throw off anybody looking to foul up the welcome wagon."

"I'll call Jack right now. Good luck."

Both Lao Ti and Lyons signed off. Lyons and Schwarz rejoined the other men in the main hallway and announced the revised plan.

"I'll get an APB out," Abko said, excusing himself.

Bronson patted his elderly client on the shoulder and told him, "I've got a few things to talk over with my people, but I'll give you a call later about the hearing, okay?"

"Gee, don't tell me you're backing out on our little joyride," Lyons taunted. "C'mon, put your neck on the line and live a little."

"I don't have time for your sarcasm," Bronson said, brushing his way past Schwarz and Lyons. "Just don't foul up on your end, and we'll hold up ours."

Left alone with Lyons and Schwarz, Felsur offered up a wry smile. "Don't mind Clovis. His bark's much worse than his bite."

"Whatever you say," Lyons said, flanking Felsur on the right while Gadgets took the left. None of the men talked the rest of the way down the corridor and through a set of security doors to the basement of an adjacent parking garage. An unmarked six-year-old Cadillac Cimarron with smoked windows was waiting for them. Schwarz climbed into the back seat, and Felsur rode shotgun while Lyons took the wheel. As agreed upon earlier, four plainclothes officers were already waiting in a pair of unmarked Plymouths. One would lead the way, while another would follow behind the Cimarron. Lyons rolled down his window and briefly explained the change of itinerary before they set out.

With the temperature down in the midtwenties, week-old snow still blanketed Cincinnati. A layer of soot and grime had tarnished the whiteness, giving the city a look of bleakness that was mirrored by the gray patchwork of clouds hovering above the entire tristate area. The roads were clear, though, and the pre-rush-hour traffic moved smoothly along the interstate. An uneasy silence continued to pervade the car's interior. Lyons drove with the flow of traffic, keeping a few lengths behind the lead Plymouth, eyes constantly inspecting the rearview mirror for any indication they were being followed by a vehicle other than the second Plymouth. In the back seat, Gadgets had his Government Model Colt .45 out of its holster and ready for use. Lyons had an identical gun tucked beneath his down jacket. Equipped with Kissinger-modified 15-round magazines and fold-down levers for two-handed shooting, the

Colts were more than capable of handling a firefight with lethal authority, but as an added precaution Lyons and Gadgets had stocked the Cadillac with impressive backup weapons, including an M-16 rifle stretched out beside Schwarz and a mini-Uzi tucked under the driver's side of the front seat.

Felsur tried to busy himself with the scenery. "This is a nice town," he said, talking to himself as much as to his bodyguards. "I'm glad I got a chance to help clean things up a little before I punch out."

"Maybe if you'd had a conscience earlier there wouldn't be as much of a mess to worry about," Lyons countered cynically.

"You got me dead to rights there, ace." The hardened street lingo sounded strange coming from the withered man. Felsur removed his glasses briefly and pulled out a handkerchief to clean the lenses. His eyes looked even smaller and more watery. Emotion made his voice hoarse. "But what's done is done. If I had it all to do over, you can bet Nash Felsur would have lived a better life. I fucked up. Real bad."

"Yeah, well, you picked a nice way to bow out of it all," Lyons said. "Cut some cushy deal and stab a few folks in the back, then walk free."

"I won't be walking much longer," Felsur reminded Lyons. "I'm on borrowed time. Maybe I can't undo all the shit I pulled, but I can at least throw in with the good guys in the last reel, eh? I wanna look my wife in the face before I croak and say my life wasn't a complete waste."

"Deathbed conversion, that it?" Lyons said. "Confess your sins and everything's okay?"

"Hey, cut me some slack, would you?" Felsur cut back. "I don't need to be kicked when I'm down, okay? You're gettin' to sound like a broken record."

Lyons gritted his teeth and vented his irritation on the steering wheel, grabbing it so hard his knuckles whitened.

"What about breaking your code of silence?" Schwarz asked the mobster. "It's not like your type to squeal, no matter what."

"Honor among thieves? Pah!" Felsur put his glasses back on and shook his head. "Maybe in the old days. Not anymore. Listen, if these young punks runnin' the show woulda played square, maybe I'd keep my lips zipped. But they got no respect for their elders. No respect for the old ways. They'd ice their mamas if there was bucks in it for 'em. Debbs, Cinzo...they're pigs!"

"Maybe so, but they still got the organization behind them, even if they're behind bars," Lyons said. "Far as you're concerned, I bet the word is you've gone soft and need to be taken out as an example to anybody else who gets ideas about stooling."

Felsur nodded gravely. "That's why you guys are here, right? You just do your job, and the cancer'll get me before they do."

"After you finish with the grand jury, what do you figure to do?" Schwarz asked the old man. "Beside taking advantage of witness relocation?"

Felsur put his glasses back on and glanced out as they passed over the Little Miami River and continued heading west. A few moments passed without Felsur answering, and Gadgets wondered if the old man's hearing was failing.

"I have a daughter." Felsur finally said. "Nan. Pretty, feisty little kid. A real looker, too. She grew up thinking her old man was some hotshot entrepreneur. I was always away on business, but whenever I came home I'd always have to give some story about the kind of work I did to afford the nice kinda life we had. She bought it all, trusting soul.

"Of course, when she got to be a teenager we had the usual problems—too much time on the phone, too many boyfriends, not enough time hitting the books. I was hard on her, but we got along, I think. She respected me, took the discipline with her chin up....''

Felsur's voice trailed off for a moment, and he licked his lips as red streaks crept across his tired eyes. Finally he was able to continue. "Then she found out I was with the mob. Musta been six, seven months ago. I was in the hospital, going through all that therapy shit. Trying to do business over the phone, using code so people couldn't figure out what the hell I was talking about. Didn't fool her, though. A couple visits and she knew the score.

"I don't know if either of you guys have kids, but there's nothing hits you like your own blood looking at you like you failed them.

"She called me names no girl that age should know, and the next day she was gone. Poof! Just took a few things, cleared out her savings account and vanished.

"We tried everything to get in touch with her. I even had a private dick lookin'—me, a fucking mobster, crawling on my knees beggin' for help. My wife bawlin' every night, hardly getting any sleep. The phone rings and we get the fucking shakes, not sure if it's her or the dick saying they found her dead somewhere. A rough time, I'm tellin' you.

"When I got out of the hospital, I stopped by this runaway center near the bus depot downtown. Nice people there, trying to put kids back in touch with their folks and vice versa. They helped us the best they could, no questions asked. Got to me, y'know? I already donated some money to them. Now I want to give 'em some time. Not here in Cincy, but wherever the wife and I end up. Maybe if we don't find Nan, we can at least help some other people out.''

"Sounds like a nice plan," Lyons said, changing lanes to keep up with the lead Plymouth. "Too bad you didn't see the light a few dozen years earlier. You might be checking out with a better ending.''

"Too bad is right," Felsur said. "Better late than never, though."

Lyons caught Gadgets's gaze in the rearview mirror. Neither man said anything, but their expressions spoke volumes. The last thing either one of them wanted was to feel pity for someone who'd spent most of his life in the mob. And yet the pathetic old man wasting away in the front seat hardly seemed dangerous; it was difficult not to be moved by his tortured soliloquy.

"You talking from the heart or is this just some schtick you've been practicing with your lawyer?" Lyons asked, bucking his inclination toward sentiment.

Felsur got that faraway look in his eyes once again. "I remember an album Nan used to play. I think it was Bruce Springman or something..."

"Springsteen," Schwarz corrected.

"Yes, that's it," Felsur said. "Well, there was one line that stuck out in my mind. Something about taking a wrong turn and just kept goin'. The story of my fucking life. I don't want my daughter to make the same mistake."

Schwarz had never been married and could only relate to the mobster's plight in vague terms. Lyons, however, had a son from a marriage that had gone on the rocks well before he'd made his way into the Stony Man operation. Although he hadn't kept up with young Tommy's growth over the years, save for a brief encounter with his ex-wife during an assignment that had indirectly involved her, he couldn't help but wonder what his son felt about him and how his absence from the boy's life had affected his upbringing. Much of what Felsur said struck home for him, and as he reached the I-75 turnoff and started south, Lyons promised himself that at the first possible opportunity he would try to get in touch with Tommy and see how he was doing.

"THAT'S THE WEIRDEST DAMN GUN I ever saw," a pasty-faced Cincinnati cop told Lao Ti as he watched her withdraw a Heckler & Koch G-11 from the trunk of her rented Alliance.

"You've never seen one of these before?" the woman asked.

"Afraid not," the cop replied, patting the stock of his .357 Colt Python. "We stick to conventional hardware in this neck of the woods."

The two of them walked away from their respective vehicles and approached a raised hillock that overlooked the Hamstead exit of Interstate 75. They tromped over the crisp, dirtied snow, seeking out the cover of a thick, rambling hedge that crowned most of the knoll. The cop's partner remained near his patrol car, keeping an eye on any traffic that might approach from the side roads linking this part of the well-to-do suburb with the highway. Since it was early afternoon, well before rush hour, there was little traffic off the interstate to be concerned with. Of course, the fact that police had quickly secured the aid of the city's Department of Transportation in posting detour signs throughout the area helped matters.

"It's made in West Germany," Lao Ti explained, holding the assault rifle out so that the cop could have a better look at it. "This plastic sheathing protects against the elements and rough handling. The sight's built into the upper handle here, and the only openings are the muzzle and ejection opening for misfires."

"What about bullet casings?" the cop wondered. "Where do they come out?"

"There aren't any casings. The bullet's set into a solid propellant. Speeds up firing a lot."

"What's a lot?"

"Two thousand rounds a minute," Lao Ti told him.

"Damn." The cop shook his head in disbelief. "Pretty impressive. But I still think I'll stick with my Colt."

As the twosome started up the knoll's slope, huge, powdery flakes of snow began falling from the thick clouds overhead. Lao Ti felt one land on her face and melt, cold on her cheek. She found it difficult to believe that a few days ago she'd been wearing short-sleeved shirts at her parents' house back in Taipei. An image of her mother and father, bedridden and feverish, briefly crept into her mind, filling her with sadness. It had been difficult for her to leave them once her sister had flown in from Hong Kong to take over their care, but she had her own life to tend to back here in the States. Trying to fill the void at Stony Man Farm left by the death of April Rose had been a considerable challenge, and she was determined to live up to the high praise that had landed her the job in the first place.

Once they had reached the top of the knoll, Lao Ti and the officer eased their way through the unwieldy brush to a vantage point that gave them a clear view of the highway and the exit ramp Felsur's three-car motorcade would be taking en route to the safehouse. The snow was coming down more heavily now, threatening a potential decrease in visibility.

Using his walkie-talkie, the cop reported his position to his partner, who was no longer in view. Then he lit up a cigarette and left the match burning a few seconds longer to warm his hands. Lao Ti reached for her communicator, figuring to touch base with both Jack Grimaldi and her two cohorts in the Cadillac. Before she could find the designated frequency, however, the woman was distracted by something that caught her eye several yards away.

"Look, over there," she whispered to her temporary partner as she shifted her grip on the assault rifle. "Fresh prints."

The cop saw the tracks and went for his Colt. There was a rustling in the brush off to their left, and before either party could react, muffled bursts of a silenced Ingram M-10 submachine gun sent a spray of .45 ACP rounds their way. Caught flat-footed, the police officer was stitched across the upper torso by at least four bullets that plowed through his heart and lungs. He followed his unfired Colt to the ground, snapping twigs under his deadweight. Blood seeped through the holes in his chest and bubbled up through his lips as his lifeless eyes glanced upward, catching snowflakes.

Lao Ti had instinctively lunged to one side, but the maneuver failed to take her completely out of the line of fire. She felt the sting of lead burrowing into her thigh, hips and midsection as she went down. Almost immediately she lost all feeling in her legs. Stunned by the unexpected assault, she nonetheless forced herself to concentrate on her options. The assault rifle had fallen beyond her reach, and she doubted that she could crawl to it in time to put it to use against the assailant she could hear coming through the brush toward her. Closing her eyes, Lao Ti tried to blot out the sensation of burning pain that raged through her and concentrate on slowing her pulse. She knew that her only chance for life at this point was to pass herself off as dead.

Through the hammering of the pain and the pounding of her heart, Lao Ti could faintly make out the sound of footsteps crunching through the snow toward her. There were whispers, two indistinguishable voices. The footsteps stopped a few yards away, where she knew the cop was lying, and then there was one cracking sound that she deduced was a bullet slamming its way through the officer's skull, ensuring that he was indeed dead.

Lao Ti knew that in a matter of seconds she would be next. The cold earth below was already red with her blood, taunting her with the realization of her mortality. She tried to will life into her legs in the remote hope that she could

ook them out there would still be others ready to
ut the assault.

went for a third option and, leaning forward,
d her trembling fingers out until they clasped the
nicator that was two feet closer to her than the rifle.
nd was shaking and her vision was clouding, but she
a deep breath and concentrated on what she was
With painstaking slowness, she fumbled with the
nicator switches until she was in a position to relay
age to Carl Lyons.

n . . . bush,'' she wheezed.

at?'' came Lyons's voice over the communicator
r. ''Lao Ti, is that you?''

nbush,'' the woman repeated, laboring over each
e. ''Off . . . ramp.''

snapped off the speaker, but one of the men had al-
heard her. As he turned from his comrade and raised
ram to take aim at Lao Ti, she summoned up the last
strength and crawled the short distance to her fallen
. There was no time to use the sights. Leveling the as-
ifle as best she could, she pulled the trigger even as she
other volley of .45 slugs pounding into her. The fog
her head turned a brilliant red. Then there was noth-

.

WICHED BETWEEN the two escort Plymouths, the
lac Cimarron exited from the highway, slowing as it
ed the cloverleaf off ramp leading to Hamstead Road.
i's warning came too late to thwart the ambush. Al-
simultaneously, two Misar MU hand grenades ex-
d on the roadway. They had been fired from different
ions by Mafia hit men brandishing Franchi SPAS
uns. Each grenade sent fifty grams of steel beads flying
t a blistering rate of 6,100 meters per second, wreak-
avoc on the tires and undercarriages of the two Ply-

lash out at her executioners with a kara
surprise maneuver. But she was still
waist, and even her upper torso seemed
mere seconds to the point where she
less. I'm going to die, she thought to he

"There!" one of the two assassins s
"Okay, let's get 'em!" a second, dee
To Lao Ti's amazement, the footstep
her, moving deeper into the brush on
facing the off ramp. She waited a few
to open her eyes. From where she was l
make out the heads and shoulders of th
whom wore light stocking caps and c
Their backs were turned to her, and she
waiting to ambush the Felsur caravan.

Steeling herself against the unsettling
ness and intense pain that seemed to rac
nating spasms, the wounded woman
slightly and found that she could roll onto
had fallen clear of the shrubs, her mov
slight sound, and neither of the assassi
her. She could see the executed policema
away from her, his face partially oblite
range blast of the Ingram.

Halfway between her and the cop, sno
ginning to cover her communicator and
Although a vague fog seemed to be cr
mind, threatening to drag her into unc
weighed her options. She could stay put,
the hope that the ambush would fail a
reached before she bled to death. Or she
within reach of the assault rifle and hope
ened state she could bring down the two
could lay siege to the motorcade. Her inst
these two men were only part of the ambu

if she
carry c
She
stretch
comm
Her ha
drew i
doing.
comm
a mess
"A
"W
speak
"A
syllab
She
ready
his In
of he
H & I
sault
felt a
inside
ing...

SANI
Cadi
roun
Lao
most
plod
direc
shot
out
ing

mouths, which had been the targeted vehicles. With their radials chewed apart, the vehicles swerved out of control for several yards before their exposed wheels bit into the asphalt and they ground to a thudding halt. Hurtling shrapnel took out windows and claimed casualties inside both autos, effectively taking them out of the action.

Lyons quickly calculated that the enemy's objective was to pin the Cadillac between the disabled Plymouths so that it would be a lame target for a follow-up assault.

"Hold on!" he shouted to Gadgets as he jerked hard on the steering wheel.

The Cadillac swerved sharply to the right, clipping the lead Plymouth and going into a brief fishtail before Lyons regained control, spitting gravel as the tires clawed at the shoulder of the off ramp. As part of a fleet of customized vehicles at the disposal of the U.S. Marshals, the Cimarron was outfitted with a number of defensive extras, including bulletproof glass and a Kevlar-reinforced body. When a hail of gunfire peppered the passenger side of the car, Nash Felsur reflexively leaned away from the side window, which took direct hits that webbed the treated glass.

"Lay down!" Lyons ordered, pressing the elderly mobster against the bench seat beside him. Although the front windshield was largely obscured from the blasts it had taken, the Ironman was still able to make out the road ahead, and he floored the accelerator, noting out of the corner of his eye that one of the ambushers had just tumbled out of a cluster of hedges atop a nearby knoll. The man crumpled to the snow and stopped moving.

"I hope that was thanks to you, Lao Ti," Lyons spit under his breath as he tried to bring the Cadillac under control and evacuate the ambush site. Any plans for escape were foiled, however, when a third grenade exploded on impact with the vehicle's front end. Although the engine block had been shielded against most forms of assault, it was no match for a direct hit from a Misar MU. The engine died at the same time the steering gave out due to a sheared tie rod on the right side. The Cadillac rolled off the road and was beginning to doughnut when it slumped down the steep incline of a ditch and came to a stop.

"Shit!" Lyons cursed, feeling a throb in his shoulder from the bite of his seat belt. He was otherwise unhurt, though, and he quickly snapped the belt loose. "Keep your ass in here, no matter what!" he commanded Felsur as he grabbed the mini-Uzi that had slid out from under his seat.

The mobster was barely conscious. A huge welt was already forming on his forehead where he'd struck the dashboard, and blood trickled where he'd bit into his lip. In the back seat, Schwarz had already holstered his .45 in favor of the M-16.

"I don't know about you, Ironman, but I'm not waiting in here for them to come get me."

"Ditto," Lyons said. His door was jammed from the crash, and he had to lean his full weight against it to get out of the car. Gadgets exited on the same side, putting them both at the base of the gully, where they were able to use the Cadillac for cover as they peered over the roof for targets.

"I just hope they're out of grenades," Gadgets wished aloud.

"I don't think so," Lyons said, swinging his mini-Uzi around and aiming in the direction of a parked police cruiser. He could see an officer lying dead next to the vehicle, and a man in camou gear loading another grenade onto his special-purpose shotgun. Well within the Uzi's 300-foot target range, the shotgunner danced the 9 mm parabellum shuffle as Lyons fired on full automatic. The Misar grenade misfired into the ground at the assassin's feet and moments later blew up, triggering a second, even more spectacular blast when the patrol car's gas tank ignited.

Meanwhile, Schwarz's keen eyes picked out a second sniper on the knoll, and he fired through the snow flurries with his M-16. A return volley of Ingram .45 ACPs thunked against the side of the Cadillac before Gadgets's bullets found their mark. Like his cohort, the gunner on the knoll was pulled into view by gravity before he slumped lifeless onto the snow-covered slope.

Yet another pair of mob hit men were still in business, firing from positions atop the servicing platform of a billboard next to the highway exit. They both had Weatherby Mark Vs, high-powered hunting rifles whose 500-grain bullets raced with a velocity that surpassed any other ammunition in the world. Even from two hundred yards, the two men pumped lead at an awesome rate of more than two thousand feet per second. Purely by accident, Lyons moved out of the first sniper's sights a split second before his head would have been crushed like a pumpkin tossed onto concrete on Halloween. The shot caromed off the Cimarron's front fender, leaving a long, deep gash in the bodywork.

"Quick, the other side!" Schwarz scrambled to the high side of the ditch, putting himself out of the sniper's sights. Lyons followed suit and plopped down in the snow. The snowfall had taken on blizzard proportions, throwing a thickening white screen around them.

"Well, they've got us pinned down," Schwarz said. "Any ideas?"

"Wait 'em out," was all Lyons could think of. "And hope they're the only ones left."

A cross-fire burst from the snipers funneled through the snow a few feet to their left. As the shots echoed in the air, they were answered by blasts both Lyons and Schwarz knew were from Government Model .45s. They waited for a rejoinder from the Weatherbys, but instead they heard the screaming of police sirens and the drone of a helicopter. And a man's voice calling out to them.

"Lyons! Schwarz! Lao Ti!"

"Music to my ears," Lyons said, lowering his mini-Uzi and clambering up to level ground. Down the road, Jack Grimaldi stood next to an AMC Jeep, still holding his Colt .45. Off to his left, one of the billboard snipers dangled stiffly at the edge of the service platform, dripping blood into the snow. The second marksman was standing erect before the billboard's oversize image of a satisfied milk drinker, his hands over his head. A police chopper hovered above him, and more officers were piling out of cruisers fresh off the interstate to assist in mopping up after the failed ambush.

"I could hear the fireworks back at the estate," Grimaldi related. "There were plenty of people there to keep an eye on the wife, so I thought I'd check things out."

"Glad you did, pal," Lyons said. "It was getting a little hairy."

"Speaking of little," Grimaldi said, glancing around, "where's Lao Ti?"

"Haven't seen her," Schwarz told the pilot.

Lyons pointed in the direction of the knoll, where two policemen were converging on the bodies of two ambushers. "I think she took out one of those guys up there."

As the three men made their way through the blizzard, more sirens announced the arrival of paramedic vans. Attendants piled out and started working on the closest victims, although it was clear theirs was a losing cause.

"Felsur's still in the Cadillac!" Lyons called out to a bloodied police officer who had climbed out of one of the wrecked Plymouths. "Better have the medics check him out, too!"

The three men shouted Lao Ti's name as they reached the top of the knoll. Receiving no reply, they split up and began wandering through the brittle hedges looking for her. It was Grimaldi who first spotted the two inert forms half-covered by freshly fallen snow. He rushed through the thickets to them and quickly saw that the cop was beyond help. Lao Ti wasn't moving, either, but when Grimaldi pressed his thumb against the woman's carotid artery, he waved to get Lyons's attention and shouted, ''Get those paramedics up here!''

6

YouRan Productions had an open part in their movie for
Veronica Rammite, and after going through the formality
of a screen test, both young women were cleared to accompany Pol Blancanales on a cross-country flight to Indianapolis Wier-Cook International Airport. They were
scheduled to arrive shortly before 1:00 p.m., but due to
drifting snow on the airstrip and low visibility caused by a
sweeping storm that had deposited more than a foot of
powder over the area, all arrivals and departures were off
schedule. It was late afternoon when they arrived with the
rest of the YouRan entourage, which also included Claudette Simms posing as Mae Jung, Otto Bendellan and a wiry
twenty-year-old gofer everyone called Scurry. Pol assumed
he'd earned the nickname because of his frenetic eagerness
to please Mae and Otto. By the time they had negotiated
rush-hour traffic out of the city and taken the crowded
freeway west to a small town called New Stanton, the sun
had gone down.

The film site was located at the edge of town, in a large
field adjacent to an abandoned rail depot. A rented cyclone fence had been erected around the property, cordon-
ing off four house trailers, five mobile homes, three
equipment trucks and the facades of several makeshift sets
that had already been erected by an advance crew that had
been in New Stanton for the better part of a week.

Once they were shown to their quarters in one of the house trailers, Maria and Veronica wearily acknowledged that they had hardly slept the night before and that exhaustion had caught up with them. Pol, who was used to sleeping under the most distressing circumstances, had enough stamina left to join Claudette Simms in her private quarters for a strategy meeting.

Pol had sat next to Claudette on the flight, and over the hours they had carried on an almost nonstop conversation. Claudette was filled with curiosity about Pol's past, and he didn't mind going over a few of the exploits he felt he could divulge without breaching security. He answered her many questions as best he could, and was flattered by her keen interest in him. And when the tables were turned and he played the part of listener, Pol found himself intrigued by the woman's climb up through the ranks of her profession, from film school through an assortment of odd jobs in which she had had to overcome prejudices against her sex to prove herself. He found it hard to believe that she had ever had problems on that front, as she exuded such an aura of poise and self-assurance. Romance had never been one of Blancanales's strong suits, and the few times he'd become involved with a woman things just hadn't worked out. But something about *this* woman struck a chord with him. He felt drawn to her, and from the signals she had given him all day, he suspected the feeling was mutual.

As he followed Claudette into the customized Winnebago, Pol felt a sudden awkwardness. Up to now, he'd been able to pass off his feelings about the woman as idle fancies, the same sort of harmless notions he often felt in restaurants or bars when he found himself eyeing women. But here he had literally crossed a threshold, and it was no longer a mere game he was caught up in.

"Drink?" Claudette asked.

"Uh, no, that's all right," Pol stammered. "Well, actually, if you have a soda or something..."

"Perrier?" she asked, opening a minirefrigerator and pulling out a small bottle of the imported spring water.

"Yeah, sure."

Blancanales caught his reflection in a mirror mounted in the narrow hallway leading to the back bedroom. Did I hear that right, Homes, he thought to himself. Pol Blancanales drinking bottled water? From France, no less? What's next, he-man? Quiche?

"Here you go, Pol."

He turned to her and accepted the drink, which had been poured into a glass and garnished with a wedge of lemon. What the hell was that for, he wondered. Fortunately, Claudette had the same drink and he followed her cue, squeezing a little of the lemon into the drink, then setting the rind aside.

"A toast?" she asked him.

"Yeah, yeah, why not?" Pol hoisted his glass. "Uh, to show business."

"There's no business like it," Claudette said, meeting his glass with her own. "To that, and to you."

She stared up at him over the rim of her glass. When she took a drink, Blancanales couldn't help but notice the way she pursed her thick, full lips, then licked them when she lowered the glass. Oh, man, Homeboy, things are moving real quick here. No wonder they call it life in the fast lane.

"So," he said, shifting his attention to the fold-out table next to the kitchenette counter. "I take it this is the layout you want me to work with, hmmm?"

He was looking at a scale model of a brick building and surrounding landscape. The attention to detail was meticulous, with each miniature tree and rock painstakingly created. Men the size of matchsticks were posted at various key locations around the main structure's perimeter, and a cutaway section of the roof showed where other men were stationed inside.

"Very realistic, don't you think?" Claudette said as she moved closer to Pol.

"I'll say." Pol took a sip of the Perrier. Damned if it didn't taste just like water with a splash of lemon. "Why all the detail?"

"It's cheaper to block out things in advance with a model than having to tie up the cast and crew for hours on end going through trial and error," Claudette explained. As she leaned forward to point at the dwarf building with her glass, her other hand crept around Pol's waist. "I was thinking that we could go over the script and start getting some ideas, okay?"

Pol discreetly moved away from Claudette and exhaled nervously. "Look, Mae, I think we're already getting ideas, if you know what I mean."

She looked at him squarely. "I like you, Pol. There's no reason why we have to keep our relationship strictly professional, is there?"

"Well, no," Pol told her. "It's just that . . . I don't know, I'm just not used to things falling into place this quick. Understand?"

There was a knock on the side door. Claudette smiled as she set down her drink. "Looks like Sam's coming to the rescue just in the nick of time, eh?" She laughed lightly and winked at Pol. "Okay, Mr. Blancanales. We'll go at your pace."

Pol was relieved. He quickly drained his French water and set the glass on the counter. Claudette opened the door and exchanged greetings with a thin man whose eyes had a strange cloudy luster. He wore a Pendleton shirt underneath a blue down vest. Claudette introduced him to Pol as Sam, the head cameraman. The two men shook hands. Blancanales had an odd feeling about Sam, but put it down to paranoia, figuring the man probably had already sized him up and slotted him as competition for the woman between them.

"Now, then, let's get to it, shall we?" Claudette said, pulling a chair away from the table and motioning for the men to do the same.

"I got some other stuff we need to discuss first," Sam told Claudette. "Private."

"Oh." Claudette turned to Pol. "Would you mind? It'll only be a minute."

"Afraid it'll be more than that," Sam said.

Pol could sense the tension Sam had brought into the trailer with him. He wasn't sure what was behind it, but he knew that he wasn't going to find out. "Tell you what," he said, plotting a graceful exit. "How about if I take this model back to my trailer and start blocking things out on my own. We can go over it in the morning."

"Thanks, Pol," Claudette said, walking him to the door. "That'll be fine. How about breakfast here at eight?"

"You got it."

Once outside, Pol paused a moment at the bottom of the steps that led down from the doorway. He could barely make out Sam's voice, although he could detect a note of urgency. Some financial problem, he guessed. Or problems with weather fouling up the shooting schedule. Whatever the case, Pol didn't feel like eavesdropping. He carried the model across the lot, which was bathed by floodlights. Scurry and a handful of other men were busy with shovels, trying to clear the day's snow from the set. A forklift stood close by, loaded with bags of rock salt that would be used to make sure the walkways wouldn't slicken with ice once they were shoveled.

Letting himself into the trailer he was sharing with Maria and Veronica, Blancanales set down the location model and checked the minifridge. It was stocked with beer and soda as well as bottled water. He cracked open a Heineken and sat down at the fold-down table. Off in the rear bedroom he could hear either Maria or Veronica snoring slightly. He grinned to himself and leaned over to switch on a portable radio on the counter. The news was just finishing, and he heard the end of a story about a shoot-out on the outskirts of Cincinnati involving police and mob figures that had left seven dead and eight critically injured. What a mess, Pol thought briefly, speculating to himself that things might have been different if his fellow Able Team members had been in on the action. A commercial came on, and he twirled the dial until he came up with some upbeat country music.

Going over the script, dividing his attention between the typed pages and the model depicting the location where the action was to take place, Blancanales slowly began tinkering with his initial strategy, taking into account new variables. He wished he had spent more time with Mae discussing what sort of weapons would be on hand for filming, as the script was extremely vague about particulars on that front. He resisted the temptation to go back to her trailer in the hope that Sam had left, figuring that Mae would misconstrue his intentions. And he had to admit she wouldn't be entirely wrong. Damn it, he couldn't seem to get that woman out of his mind. Whenever his attention strayed from the script, even for a moment, he suddenly heard Mae's voice, her laughter, and smelled the subtle perfume she wore. Ah, those lips, Homes. Imagine the things she could do with those lips. And those fingers. Long, slender, graceful. Imagine them slowly working at the buttons of her blouse, as her green eyes take you in, daring you to come closer as her voice slowly purrs your name....

"Rosario. Rosario."

Pol stirred slightly, then snapped upright in his chair. Veronica Rammite stood before him in her housecoat, eyeing him with concern. Light was pouring through the trailer windows, and Pol quickly surmised that he'd fallen asleep at the table. The script was open in his lap, and the set model lay before him. Across the room, Maria was on her way to answer a knock at the door.

"Good morning, Maria," Claudette greeted Pol's sister. "Ready for action?"

"I think so."

"I'm looking for your brother," Claudette said. "He stood me up for breakfast."

"In here," Pol called out, blinking the sleep from his eyes. He stood up, rubbing his lower back where it had stiffened on him during the night. His injured leg was still asleep, and he had to lean against the counter to wait for the tingling to subside. One look at Mae in her fur-lined parka and he remembered what he'd been thinking about when he dozed off. "Sandman nailed me when I wasn't looking," he apologized. "Sorry."

"That's okay," Claudette said. Seeing the model, she asked, "Did you manage to come up with something?"

Pol nodded. "There are still a few loose ends to work out, but I've got a handle on it."

"Good. I'm rounding up the troops for a dry run in about an hour. You'll be ready by then?"

"Sure," Pol promised.

Claudette smiled at the two younger women. "Since it's just a rehearsal, you can bundle up in whatever you like. Your costumes won't be in till later this afternoon, anyway."

"Costumes?" Maria asked.

Claudette nodded. "We have to hire people to handle everyone's wardrobe. Union regulations."

"Oh, right, of course."

"See you soon, then." Claudette slipped a quick wink at Pol before leaving. Maria caught it as well.

"So, brother dearest," she teased, "cozying up to the boss, are you?"

Pol yawned, pretending not to hear. Heading for the bathroom, he said, "I think I'll grab a quick shower. You girls through in there?"

Maria and Veronica raided the bathroom for their make-up and rollers, then let Pol have the room to himself. A few minutes under near-scalding water loosened up his back and washed away some of his jet lag. When he changed and came back out, the girls had made coffee and toast. They were dressed for the day and sitting next to each other on a Naugahyde couch, going over the script. Both of them had a look of disappointment.

"Can you believe it? We're only in two scenes!" Maria complained. "And I only have three lines."

"That's one more than I have," Veronica said.

"And it's three more than me," Pol added with a grin. "Look, ladies, you gotta start somewhere, right? It's not like you beat out Meryl Streep to get here."

Veronica got up to use the bathroom. Maria sighed and closed the script. "You're right . . . like always."

"I wouldn't go quite that far," Pol said. "And if you don't believe me, just ask Pops."

"Hey, Daddy thinks a lot of you," Maria told her brother. "You should hear the way he brags about you all the time." She stood up and changed her posture, hunching her shoulders slightly and jutting her chin forward in a gesture that was pure Jorges Blancanales. Doing her best to imitate her father's voice, she said, "My Rosario, he's a hero like John Wayne. Yeah, that's my boy, the Mexican John Wayne!"

Pol laughed between bites of toast. "Come off it, Sis. He never said anything like that."

"Cross my heart," Maria said. "I just think he butts heads with you all the time because he's got his pride. You know, he's gotta be the big man around the house."

Blancanales took a lined overcoat from his suitcase and shook his head with amusement as he put it on. "You taking psychology between acting classes, Sis?"

"Tease me all you want, but you know I'm right on this one." She stepped forward and gave her brother a playful punch on the shoulder. "And I'm right about you having the hots for Mae, too."

"Whatever you say, Pixie. Whatever you say." When Veronica rejoined them, Pol headed for the door and held it open. "Now let's go grab our slice of 'Lifestyles of the Rich and Famous,' okay?"

Outside, the storm front had passed, and steam rose from the ground as sunlight fell across the film set. Most of the snow had been cleared away and shoveled into a tall heap at the corner of the lot. Half a dozen men were standing in front of the old depot, and another group was gathered around a propane heater with Claudette, Otto Bendellan and Scurry the gofer.

Claudette introduced Pol to the men, who included her Wyoming flunkies Rudy and Jimbo, explaining, "These guys make up the Delta Force."

Pol kept a straight face as he took in the men with a sweeping gaze. They were big in build, but clearly out of shape. Delta Force, my ass, he thought to himself. On the whole, these guys didn't look as if they could last through more than a couple of hours of the kind of training the real troopers were used to. He guessed they'd have better luck enduring a Delta frat mixer, but he kept the opinion to himself.

"Okay, Iranians!" Claudette called out to the men near the depot. "Take up your positions."

Apparently the actors playing the Iranians would be wearing brownface during shooting, because they were all very pale-skinned. As they started for their designated spots, Pol caught Claudette's attention. "You know, I think realistically the depot would be defended differently from the way it's blocked out right now," he informed her.

"Oh, that's okay," Claudette insisted. "We set those positions up because they make for the best camera angles. Sam's already got those shots figured out, and we're too rushed to change that. It's the Delta Force's moves that we're more concerned about."

"I'm a little confused," Maria said as she warmed her hands over the burner. "This scene doesn't take place until the end of the movie. How come we're doing it first?"

"Money." Claudette smiled indulgently and gave Maria a quick crash course in a cardinal element of film production. "It just doesn't make sense in terms of logistics to shoot a movie in the same order as the scenes appear in the script. Why, we'd have people in one scene twiddling their thumbs for days waiting for their next camera call, and the budget would go through the roof. That's why we're starting off with the climax. It's the only scene we need all these people for at the same time. Once we've filmed it and know how much it cost us, we'll have a better idea of how to schedule the rest of the shooting. Make sense?"

Maria nodded. "Yeah. I guess I could have figured that out myself if I'd thought about it."

"No problem. The best way to learn things in this business is to ask questions. Don't be embarrassed, okay?"

"As long as we're on the subject of budget," Pol said, "I need to know what kind of arrangements you're making for weapons. That's going to determine what kind of strategy the Deltas would use."

Claudette pounded her forehead lightly with the butt of her palm. "I can't believe I forgot to give you that info yesterday. Otto, do you have the list on you?"

Bendellan nodded and went through his pockets for a slip of paper. He showed it to Pol. "This is an inventory from a studio supply house. We can get anything on this list, along with blank ammunition, of course."

Blancanales raised an eyebrow as he surveyed the list, which offered quite a smorgasbord of death-dealing ordnance, from C-4 plastic explosives and anti-armor Vipers to more conventional M-16s and Colt Commandos. If he wanted to, Pol felt, he could put together an arsenal capable of leveling the entire depot and all "Iranians" within a fifty-yard radius, but he was determined, despite Mae's penchant for expediency, to strive for realism as much as possible. Relying on his own knowledge of Delta Force armaments and taking into account the layout of the depot and the intent of the mission, he quickly calculated the type of weapons he wanted and scribbled notations on the "grocery list" Bendellan had given him.

"I think this should cover it," he told Otto as he handed the list back.

Bendellan and Claudette both looked over the sheet with deadpan expressions. Then Otto folded it up and slipped it back in his pocket. "I'll go check this out against our budget and see if we can swing it."

"Do that," Claudette said. "In the meantime, Pol, will you take these guys and lead them through their paces? Sam will be by shortly and he can figure out if everything will play on film."

"Gotcha." Leaving Maria and Veronica behind, Pol led Rudy, Jimbo, and the other would-be Special Forces over to the facade of a building located almost seventy yards away from the depot. "Okay," he told them, "according to the script, you get to this point by crawling up through the sewers, and now you'll want to start spreading out...."

As Blancanales choreographed the action sequence, a burgundy Lincoln Continental rolled onto the film lot and came to a stop near the house trailers. Claudette and Otto walked over to the driver's side of the vehicle. Inside, Dave X. Fabyan rolled down the window. He was scowling.

"I heard on the news," Otto told the mobster. "Things didn't go too well in Cincy, did they?"

"You're goddamn right they didn't," Fabyan snarled. "Jesus, I lost half my best men, and I gotta worry that the one they got alive will sing to save his ass! What a fucking mess!"

"Well, at least things are shaping up on our end," Otto said, retrieving the weapons list. "If you can get this shit for us by tomorrow, I think we'll be ready to make our hit."

Fabyan cooled off as he browsed the list. "Shouldn't be a problem. I'll give Nevrut a ring and head down there after lunch." He looked at Claudette. "You wanna join me, Claudette?"

She shook her head and smirked. "Sorry, but I got a new boyfriend." She glanced over his shoulder at Pol, who had Rudy and Jimbo crawling across the cold ground on their hands and knees. "Wouldn't want him to get jealous, now, would we?"

"No, I guess not. In that case, I'll head out."

Fabyan shifted into reverse, but before he could pull away, Bendellan leaned toward the window and asked, "Did you at least get Felsur's present to him?"

Fabyan looked at the clock on the Lincoln's dashboard. "He oughta be gettin' it right about now...."

7

As city crews took to the streets to plow snow and right power lines that had fallen during the past ten hours, Cincinnati General Hospital buzzed with a crowd of patients suffering from various injuries sustained in traffic accidents directly attributable to the treacherous weather.

There were also the casualties of the "Shoot-out at Hamstead Road"—the media's reference name for the previous afternoon's bloodbath. Most of the victims were across town at the county morgue, but three wounded police officers had been hospitalized, two with shrapnel wounds from the Misar grenades and one with a .45 bullet wedged between his shattered rib and a perforated lung. All three were on the critical list but were expected to survive.

The same couldn't be said for Lao Ti. The loss of blood alone had nearly been fatal, and the fact that slugs from the Ingram submachine gun had riddled her body in nearly a dozen places had tipped the scales further against her. She had already been in surgery several times, and had spent a total of thirteen hours under the knife. The various monitors she was hooked up to in the private intensive care room gave a clear indication that she was hanging on to life by the finest of threads.

Out in the waiting room, Carl Lyons sat rigidly on an uncomfortable sofa, oblivious to a dozen other people holding their own vigils for loved ones. He'd been there for some time, slowly digesting the grim prognosis given him earlier by the chief of surgery.

"That she's still with us at all is a miracle," the man had told him. "I suggest you get in touch with her next of kin and have them prepare for any necessary arrangements."

Damn it, she couldn't die, Lyons told himself. It was just too fucking unfair. Although he'd never really had a chance to get close to Lao Ti during the short time she'd been assigned to Stony Man Farm, Lyons couldn't help but lump her in with the other women he had cared about, so many of whom had fallen victim to the forces of evil in the world. Only a few months had passed since he'd lost his beloved Julie Harris, and before her there had been Margaret Williams and Flor Trujillo and April Rose. It was almost as if he were a lethal Midas, bringing death to any female he touched. It wasn't fair. Goddamn it, it just wasn't fair.

Across from Lyons, a man in his fifties stubbed out the latest in a chain of half-smoked cigarettes and dragged his fingers through his thinning hair. There was fatigue in his eyes, and he looked at Lyons as if seeking a kindred spirit. "Why?" he croaked hoarsely through his smoke-ravaged throat. "One minute my wife is putting groceries in the car, the next some drunk in a pickup spins out and crushes her legs. Why do these things happen?"

Lyons wasn't in the mood to coddle someone else's misery. "Life is hard and then you die," he told the man matter-of-factly, trying to force himself to face up to the ultimate truism that always seemed to govern his behavior. He got up from his chair and headed for the row of phone booths in the adjacent lobby.

"Hey, thanks a lot for the cheering up," the other man called after him sarcastically. "I really needed that."

Lyons paused in the doorway and glared back. "Look, I'm sorry. But if you want cheering up, maybe you should try the circus."

The Ironman strode into the lobby without waiting for a response. He was angry with himself for having shot his mouth off, but the anger was going to have to pick a number and wait before he'd be able to deal with it. There were other things on his mind now.

Closing himself off inside one of the phone booths, he made a quick series of calls that finally put him in touch with Aaron Kurtzman, Stony Man's wheelchair-bound communications wizard. The two men had already spoken shortly after the firefight outside of town, and when Lyons relayed the chief of surgery's mention of next of kin, there was a brief pause on Kurtzman's end of the line.

"You still there, Bear?" Lyons asked.

"Yeah," Kurtzman said. "Look, Carl, I really don't think I can put through that call to Taiwan, at least not yet. I… Lao Ti's sister just called here this morning trying to get in touch with her. Their father passed away yesterday afternoon. The mother's nearly out of her mind with grief, and she's not all that well herself."

"Shit," Lyons muttered, slapping his hand in frustration against the thick glass of the booth's door. "When it rains it fucking pours, doesn't it?"

"Afraid so," Kurtzman replied. "Listen, Carl. Last night you said Felsur was going to check photos of the people that staged the ambush to see if he could name names. Any luck on that, at least?"

"Yeah," Carl muttered. "He pegged them all as soldiers working for some guy named Dave X. Fabyan. He's *caporegime* for Pete Cinzo, part of the Cleveland family Felsur sends upriver if he talks."

"Thanks to you guys, it looks like that's gonna happen, right?"

"I guess so," Lyons said. "Schwarz and Grimaldi are back at the house with Felsur and his wife and half the goddamn Ohio National Guard. They're going to bring the frigging jury to Felsur. Seems to me we've done our part.''

Kurtzman sighed on the other line. "Afraid that's not the way the chief sees it.''

"Why did I know you were going to say that?''

"Brognola wants you to remain in Cincinnati on a standby basis. From all the intelligence we've been able to tap into, it just doesn't look like things are close to being over out there. We might need you guys to take the offensive.''

"Well, that's a different story,'' Lyons said, his spirits rising slightly. He knew from experience that when it came to tackling the mob, one's best bet was to dig in and beat them at their own game rather than wait to react to whatever shit they might hit the fan with. In light of what had happened to Lao Ti, he was particularly eager to take whatever action possible to hack his way through Cosa Nostra underlings to the upper echelons of the organization, where some real harm could be done. "Just give us the green light, Bear, and we'll lay into those bastards so hard they'll be lining up behind Felsur to kiss the D.A.'s ass.''

"I'm sure you'd do that,'' Kurtzman said, "but until you get that green light, just stay put, okay?''

"I'm going to drive myself stir-crazy,'' Lyons complained. Remembering one bit of unfinished business, he asked Kurtzman, "What about this Abko character? You get a sheet on him?''

"Yeah, and his record's clean. He's been a marshal going on ten years, and no infractions. Word is he's got a short fuse and doesn't put much stock in glad-handing.''

"I could have told you that,'' Lyons said, recalling his verbal exchange with the marshal earlier. "And he's got no mob ties?''

"Zip... well, not unless you go back fifteen years. Says here he worked vice squad for a full stint as a cop up in

Cleveland. That doesn't necessarily mean that he dealt with the mob, but—"

"Oh, come off it, Bear," Lyons scoffed. "You work vice in a big city, you get to know the mob."

"Still, that was a long time ago."

"Yeah, maybe so, but at least it's something to go on. Beats the hell out of twiddling my thumbs at the hospital. I'm gonna run with it."

"As long as you know the chief hasn't cleared it."

"You don't tell him and he won't have to know about it, right, Bear?"

"That's not the way we work, Carl." Kurtzman gently chided. "People have a way of making a lot of noise when *you* lean on them."

"Let me worry about that," Lyons said. "I'm outta here."

"Good luck," the Bear told him. "And let's all keep pulling for Lao Ti."

"Right."

Lyons hung up the phone and checked at the waiting room for any new developments with Lao. Her condition was unchanged, which was good news as far as the doctors were concerned.

The man Lyons had exchanged words with earlier was nowhere to be seen. His seat had been taken by another worried man going through the same ritual of constantly checking the doors to the operating wing and trying not to let his anxiety overwhelm him. Lyons wasn't about to pass along another succinct sermon on the inequities of life. He wanted to save his breath for someone else.

ABE ABKO LEFT the U.S. Marshals' office and, as he did most weekday nights, strolled across the street to Dawn Juan's, a yuppie-oriented Mexican bar that served an ample happy-hour buffet and was a prominent meeting place for singles from nearby law firms and corporations. The beefy officer commandeered his favorite seat at the bar and placed an order for a double margarita before venturing to the buffet table and loading up a small plate with miniature *fajitas*, chips, salsa, guacamole dip, and deep-fried chicken wings. He tried to start up some small talk with a winsome young woman who'd come to the table for a carrot stick, but she gave him the cold shoulder and headed back to join three other office workers in a corner booth.

"Your loss, honey," Abko consoled himself, biting into a chip.

"Whaddya know," Carl Lyons said, appearing on the other side of the buffet table. "Small town, huh?"

Abko recognized Lyons and sneered. "Too fucking small, if you ask me."

"Hey, a little less venom, Abe, buddy." Lyons grinned, scooping spiced meatballs onto an hors d'oeuvre plate. "This is supposed to be happy hour, right?"

"You wanna make me happy, go play in the traffic."

"Already did that." Lyons followed Abko back to the bar and slipped onto the empty stool next to him. He motioned to the bartender that he wanted a margarita as well, then told Abko, "Play got a little rough, too."

"So I heard."

"Funny thing is, that whole transfer with Felsur was changed at the last minute," Lyons reflected. "The way those guys set up the ambush, they had to have some advance warning that we were coming the way we did."

Abko talked as he stacked fixings on his minitortilla. "After I put out the APB, anybody coulda tipped things off." He bit savagely into his *fajita*, then washed it down with half his margarita. He wiped his lips with a napkin and glared at Lyons. "You wanna point a finger at me, you better have something to back it besides hot air."

"Let's talk about Cleveland," Lyons said, slipping the bartender four bucks for his drink. "I hear you did a little badge work on the vice beat up there."

"Yeah, fifteen years ago," Abko said. "One partner got syph, another decided he'd like pimping for the mob until they found out he was skimming and gave him a .22 bypass, if you get my drift."

"And you got through it with your halo intact, is that it?"

Abko drained his drink and ordered another, then told Lyons, "You already did your homework, you should know."

"That hit on Hamstead Road was courtesy of a guy named Fabyan. Ring a bell?"

"Yeah. Did a lot of them beach movies with that Mouse-keteer I always wanted to slip it to. Annette, right?"

"Guess again. This Fabyan's from Cleveland."

Abko shrugged. "Like you said, small world, huh?"

"You don't remember him, though?"

Abko's patience was at an end. "Look, G-boy, I'm off duty," he said, leaning across the bar to face off with Lyons. "I got a feeling you are, too, so how's about we knock off the shop talk before you make me really mad?"

Lyons finished his drink and got down off his stool. "Okay. But I'm on to you, Abe baby. I got a partner at Cincy General about to cash in her chips, and if she goes, your fat ass is—"

"Nobody threatens me!" Abko roared, kicking his stool out from under him as he lunged for Lyons.

There were shrieks throughout the bar as the two men tussled at close quarters. Abko was as strong as he was big, and Lyons wasn't able to wriggle clear enough of the mar-shal's grip to effectively counter with any karate moves. Like a disoriented four-legged beast, the linked men bounded over several fixtures and off one of the walls before losing their balance and tumbling headlong into the buffet table.

Appetizers went flying in all directions as the men went down.

By now management was on the scene, and the night manager sent four busboys, the bartender and three waiters into the fray in an effort to restore order. Although they clearly outnumbered the two combatants, it took all eight men the better part of a minute to pry Lyons away from Abko.

"Outside!" Abko shouted at Lyons, blood trailing from a cracked lip. "I'll get an apology out of you if I have to break every goddamn bone in your body!"

Lyons rubbed his jaw where he'd caught a stray elbow during the skirmish. He gestured for the four men holding him to let go, then straightened out his disheveled clothes. "Tell you what," he told Abko. "You want me to take it back, you find whoever leaked my orders to Fabyan's goons."

"Not good enough," Abko insisted. "I want an apology! Now!"

"Sorry," Lyons said, directing his remarks to the restaurant manager. He gave the man a business card with an unlisted number that would put him in touch with the dummy accounting firm that handled Stony Man's unexpected expenses. "They'll see to it that you're taken care of."

Ignoring Abko's continued howls, Lyons left the bar and drove the Jeep back to the country mansion where Nash Felsur and his wife were being held. They were under the most protective custody of any individuals in the nation aside from those occupying the White House.

And yet, despite the veritable army of personnel watching over the estate, the Mafia had still found a way to get to Nash Felsur and hurt him where it counted.

As Lyons walked past the gauntlet of National Guardsmen pulling sentry duty in front of the house and into the hallway, he could hear an almost hideous cry of pure and absolute despair. It was a woman's voice, and when Lyons traced it to the den he saw Nash Felsur clinging tightly to his fifty-year-old wife. He himself was weeping and seemed on the verge of joining her in a display of uncontrolled hysteria.

Jack Grimaldi was in the den, and when he spotted Lyons he walked out and led his companion into the nearby kitchen.

"What happened?" Lyons wanted to know.

"They just got a package delivered to them," Grimaldi said, gesturing to an unwrapped box on the kitchen counter.

Lyons slowly walked over to the counter, still hearing Julia Felsur's anguished cries in the next room. The box was square and made of thick plastic, big enough for a bowling ball. Lyons felt an uneasiness in his stomach as he pulled away the lid, wary of what he was going to see. There was no way he could have been fully prepared for the sight.

Inside the box was Nan Felsur's mutilated, severed head, resting in half-melted ice, facing upward with unseeing eyes. The color of her flesh had already changed drastically. On her forehead, someone had carefully carved a message in the skin: *YOUR WIFE'S NEXT.*

Lyons quickly turned away from the box, feeling a surge of rage burn through the queasiness in his stomach. It was not the first time someone had resorted to such hideous tactics. "Animals," he said. "They're fucking animals."

"Especially when you consider she was killed before the attempted hit down the road," Grimaldi told him. "It just turned out to be a handy coincidence that they could send it here as a threat. She was killed for kicks."

8

By conservative estimate, more than twenty million dollars worth of ordnance winds up missing from military bases and depots throughout the U.S. every year. Some of that total is unaccounted for due to human error, as in the case of accidental inventory discrepancies, inaccurate measuring techniques at firing ranges, shipping irregularities and related mishaps. But more often, the cause is human design. Inherent flaws in supply and delivery systems, lax inspection procedures, inadequate security precautions—there are countless factors that make it possible for anyone with enough greed, determination or influence to tap into the nation's arsenal and help himself to a variety of weapons. Although outside raiders are responsible for some of this illicit loss, the alarming majority of these munitions heists are masterminded by insiders—men who engage in their clandestine pursuits while members of the Armed Forces.

Men like Navy supply officer Eddie Nevrut.

As a trusted official at the Crane Naval Ammunition Depot, an hour's drive south of New Stanton, Nevrut knew the ins and outs of ordnance transportation to and from the facility. If there was something he didn't understand about operations, he was always eager to ask around until he found answers, always appearing to have the Navy's best interests at heart. His fellow officers were impressed by Nevrut's zeal for the job, especially when he had enlisted for a second Navy hitch after he'd already served four years.

None of them suspected that he was using his position as a springboard for his closet career as one of the Midwest's most reliable underground suppliers of commercially unavailable weapons.

Off duty for the day, Nevrut changed into civilian togs and, as he did four or five times a week, drove his restored and customized '43 Chevy pickup through the depot gates, treating security officers there to the latest obscene joke making the rounds at the compound. Once on the country roads, he cranked up the radio and hummed along to a heartbreaking ballad by Lee Greenwood. In his mind he was juggling figures, trying to calculate how much he was going to clear on today's deal. Let's see—five M-249s, two Mark 19 MOD-3 grenade launchers, two 400-round box magazines, two Colt Commandos, four .44 AutoMags—a lotta moola, no matter how you slice it, all cash on the barrelhead.

After twenty minutes, Nevrut pulled off the main road and engaged the Chevy's newly installed four-wheel drive as he powered his way up a snow-covered driveway that cut through the woods that formed part of Hoosier National Forest. Off to his left he saw a young buck dart through the trees. One of these days he was going to have to take some time off and do some serious hunting with one of his pilfered Weatherbys.

A few hundred yards in from the road, Nevrut came upon a gateway and a cyclone fence topped with deadly swirls of barbed wire. He idled the Chevy before the gate and climbed out, going through his pockets for a second set of keys. He sprang a lock and unwrapped the length of chain holding the gate closed. It took his full weight and a fervent shove to swing the gate in over the snow, and he grunted at the exertion.

To his amazement, as he was pausing to catch his breath the officer heard the Chevy's gears mesh. He spun around and saw his pickup heading toward him. Scurry the gofer was behind the wheel. Dave X. Fabyan stood alongside the vehicle, a Smith & Wesson .357 in his hand, pointed Nevrut's way.

"Hey, guys," Eddie called out, trying not to show his unease. "What gives? I thought we were meeting at my trailer, like always."

"We always wondered where your warehouse was, Eddie," Fabyan said as he climbed up onto the pickup's running board. "How about if you play hood ornament and lead the way?"

"What?"

Fabyan fired the Smith & Wesson into the snow between Nevrut's legs, then raised the gun's barrel a few inches higher. The cheerful singsong had left his voice. "Get your fucking ass up on the hood...and put your hands on your head while you're at it."

Nevrut reluctantly complied with the mobster's orders, stepping up onto the front bumper and then swinging around so that he was seated on the hood. He could feel the engine's warmth beneath him. As the truck inched forward, the officer tried to think back and recall if any vehicle had followed him from the depot. Not that it mattered. One way or another, they'd found him out, and he knew that once he'd served his purpose as tour guide of his private weapons cache he was a dead man...unless he could somehow get to the Detonics .45 tucked between his belt and his briefs.

"I've always dealt with you fair and square," he said, turning slightly to one side so Fabyan could hear him. "Why the shakedown?"

"Business, Eddie," Fabyan told him. "No need to take it personal."

Nevrut couldn't help but laugh. "Oh, really? My own fucking property you fuck me over on, and I'm not supposed to take it personal? Get real."

They were coming up on an old, weather-worn barn with a faded advertisement for chewing tobacco barely visible on the south side.

"What do we have here?" Fabyan wondered aloud. "Looks kinda like Claudette's joint up in Wyoming, eh, Scurry?"

Scurry the gofer nodded at his boss from behind the wheel. "Sure thing. Probably has just as many surprises inside, too, huh?"

There was a padlock on the main entrance to the barn, and snow drifted up at a pitched angle against the doors. Off to one side, Fabyan could make out the handle of a snow shovel propped against the wall.

"Get down and start shoveling," Fabyan ordered Nevrut.

"Be kinda hard to do with my hands on my head, don't you think?" Eddie complained.

"Just do it!" Through the trees, Fabyan could see the sun dropping quickly toward the horizon. He wanted to wrap things up and be on the way back to New Stanton by dusk. "Scurry, you help."

Scurry put the Chevy in neutral and climbed down, letting Fabyan take his place behind the wheel. Eddie jumped down from the hood and grabbed the shovel, laying into the snow with fierce determination. Scurry made use of a slab of wood as a makeshift shovel and began whittling away at the drift in front of the doors.

Nevrut pretended to be engrossed in his menial task, but he kept stealing glances at both men, trying to gauge his best opportunity for taking action. He worked his way closer to Scurry, then shifted his weight slightly. In a quick, fluid one-two motion, he pitched a shovelful of snow against the windshield of his Chevy, then jerked the shovel back in the opposite direction, ramming the handle into Scurry's midsection. The gofer doubled over, wheezing for air. Nevrut pulled out his .45 and circled around Scurry, using the man as a human shield between himself and Dave X. Fabyan.

The moment the snow had come flying against the Chevy's windshield, Fabyan had leaned away from the steering wheel. The action saved his life, as a bullet subsequently shattered the glass and flattened itself against the chassis frame directly behind the driver's seat.

Fabyan slid across the seat and pushed open the front passenger door, then squirmed out of the vehicle, easily staying clear of a second shot from Nevrut's Detonics. When the mobster peered over the front fender, he saw that Eddie was still standing behind Scurry and was now holding the .45 to the gofer's head.

"Get away from the truck!" Nevrut commanded. "Just let me go and you can take what you want."

"I plan to, Eddie."

Fabyan squeezed off three shots from his Smith & Wesson, drilling holes through Scurry the gofer in order to get at the Naval officer. Nevrut's .45 went off as he died, blowing away half of Scurry's head. Both men crumpled to the snow.

Fabyan calmly walked over to the bodies and frisked Nevrut for the keys to the barn. Throwing the doors open, he stepped into the enclosure and gawked as the twilight fell upon Eddie Nevrut's private stock, a hoard of weapons and ammunitions so plentiful that Fabyan quickly estimated he'd need at least two semis to clear it all out.

"Jackpot," he murmured.

9

"Oh, come on, you've got to be kidding!"

Maria Blancanales held up the short leather skirt and gold spindle top that Claudette had just handed to her. A few feet away, Veronica Rammite looked over an equally skimpy outfit. The three women were in Claudette's private Winnebago.

"No, not at all," Claudette said. "You're supposed to be distracting the guards, after all, aren't you?"

"Yes, but, Ms. Jung...really! This is the eighties," Maria protested. "Can't we do it with a little less exploitation?"

"Yeah," Veronica seconded, "like we could dress up nice and play it like we're executive secretaries just out for a fling. We don't *have* to be prostitutes, do we?"

The door behind them opened, and Otto Bendellan climbed up into the unit. Claudette looked at the two fledgling actresses, clearly struggling to remain patient. She finally gave in. "Okay. I'll make you a deal. If you play it out the way it's in the script first and we end up with some extra time later, we'll do a few more takes and try it your way. That's the best I can offer."

Maria and Veronica looked at one another. Both suspected that there was little likelihood of them getting their way, but neither felt like pressing the issue any further. Maria nodded, draping her costume over her arm and heading past Otto for the door.

"Come on, Ronnie," she told her friend with a trace of sarcasm, "let's practice jiggling."

Veronica played along. "Good idea. Maybe if we're lucky they can find a way to have us walk over heating vents so these skirts will ride up our legs."

"Don't put ideas in our heads," Claudette chuckled.

Otto held the door open for the girls, letting them out into the cold Indiana night. He watched them briefly as they walked across the quiet lot, then closed and locked the door. Turning to Claudette, he smiled. "Mutiny of the prima donnas?"

Claudette shrugged. "They'll get their chances to be leading ladies soon enough. Louie come through for us?"

Otto tapped a manila envelope he was carrying. "Right here." He withdrew a handful of documents and gestured for Claudette to have a look. There were registration forms for film equipment, titles to the mobile unit and other vehicles on the lot, corporation filings for a film production company, and a half dozen other permits and titles—all of them forged.

All of them contained the simulated signature of Rosario Blancanales.

"Very good," Claudette said as she inspected the paperwork. "Louie's gotten better at this lately, don't you think?"

"Amazing what a guy can do with the right incentive," Otto cracked. "And this isn't even the best news. I just got a call from Fabyan. You aren't going to believe this. He says Nevrut had enough hardware stashed near the depot to arm all our people from here to the Rockies. A fucking mother lode. Hell, we could almost shine this whole thing at Terre Haute."

"Did Fabyan say that?" Claudette asked, arching her eyebrows.

"No," Otto confessed. "He wants to go ahead with it as scheduled."

"Good," Claudette said. She rustled the forged papers. "After all this preparation I'd really hate to walk away from it."

"He said he'll bring up the weapons Blancanales asked for in the morning."

"I hope it's first thing, because I want to have at least two or three run-throughs to make sure we have things down pat." Claudette reached behind her neck and rubbed at the base of her skull, grimacing slightly. "Damn, just what I don't need is a headache."

"Let me do that for you." Otto came up behind Claudette and began to massage her neck. She groaned pleasurably, swaying her head from side to side.

"Oh, that's nice. Listen, is Scurry coming back up tonight? There's a few things I need him to—"

"Claudette," Otto interrupted, "there were a few complications when they surprised Nevrut."

There was a pause. Claudette stiffened. Her skin paled.

"Scurry's dead," she guessed.

"Afraid so."

"Damn it!"

"I'm sorry."

Claudette crossed her arms in front of her, tensing the entire length of her body. The expression on her face was less one of grief than of angry disappointment. "I wanted him tonight," she whispered. "I really needed it."

Otto moved closer to Claudette, pressing his chest against her back and letting his hands trail from her neck down her arms. His lips brushed lightly against her ear and his tongue crept out, curling itself moistly around her lobe. "I've seen the films of you and him," he murmured seductively. "I can do those things for you, too."

Claudette cringed for a moment in Otto's arms, then pulled herself away and lashed out with her hand, slapping him across the face. "Bastard!" she hissed. "How dare you invade my privacy like that!"

Otto grinned at the woman as he rubbed his reddened cheek. "Very good, bitch!" he teased. "But I know you can do better."

She swung at him again, but this time he caught her by the wrist and quickly pinned her arm behind her back. She winced, grabbing between his legs with her free hand.

"Come on, let's get to your bed and I'll make you forget him forever!" Otto told her, pressing himself against her.

He shoved her down the narrow hallway leading to a small bedroom, then changed his grip, closing the fingers of both hands softly around her upper arms. Otto felt her relax against him, and he knew she was looking forward to the evening as much as he was.

POL BLANCANALES WAS STRETCHED OUT on a couch in the trailer he shared with Veronica and Maria, who were in the back bedroom devising schemes for turning their brief screen appearances into cinematic moments they could build careers on. He could overhear some of their revised dialogue, and it was all he could do to keep from laughing aloud. Their idea of witty one-liners made the already mediocre lines in the script sound like Shakespeare.

Despite their complaints about having to play streetwalkers, Pol sensed that the girls were enjoying themselves. So was he, for that matter. It had been a long day, constantly working and reworking the placement of men and the sequence of activities in the scene that would be the climax of *You Ran, Iran*. In the absence of actual weapons or even reasonable facsimiles, sticks had been used for guns and rifles, snowballs for grenades. Although the actual strategy and circumstances in the movie took their cues from

Pol's real-life exploits with Able Team, the prop ordnance
and the constant breaks to restage certain movements reminded him more of childhood warfare, when he and other
kids in the neighborhood had found themselves a suitable
mock battlefield and proceeded to spend hours engaged in
fantasized conflict. Just as today's maneuvers had been put
on hold with the arrival of a vending van stocked with lunch
offerings, so had the monumental sieges in San Ysidro and
East Los Angeles ended whenever mothers rang dinner bells
or some kid got roughed up and went home crying.

And then there was Mae. No kid's game on that front.
They had continued flirting with one another throughout
the day, trading their mutual attraction. Pol had suggested
that they take off after sundown, use one of the cars and
drive into town for a nice dinner. But she had begged off,
saying that there were always a million preproduction details to be ironed out the day before shooting.

The trailer came equipped with an old portable black-and-
white television set, and Pol switched from channel to
channel looking for something interesting to watch. One
station was broadcasting news, and he caught a story about
the sensational events surrounding mob informant Nash
Felsur's pending grand jury testimony against several high-
ranking syndicate underbosses currently in police custody in
Cincinnati. An on-the-scene reporter standing outside the
Hamilton County Courthouse stared out at Blancanales and
divulged that security for the ailing Felsur had been inten-
sified in the wake of an attempt on the mobster's life and
Felsur's receipt of a box containing the head of his daughter.

Blancanales quickly switched off the television, but he
was far less successful clearing the news story from his mind.
It brought back too many bad memories of the unspeakable cruelties that depraved men could inflict upon a cap-

tive woman. His older sister, Toni, had been raped in Minneapolis.

"Hey, big boy, wanna party?"

Pol snapped out of his reverie and glanced across the room to where Veronica was leaning seductively against the trailer wall, a tight skirt riding halfway up her thighs when she moved one leg. A sleeveless beaded sweater left little doubt as to the extent of her postadolescent development. She was grinning awkwardly at Blancanales, and finally she broke out laughing, her face turning red with embarrassment. Maria strode into view in her outfit and modeled briefly for her brother.

"Can you believe she actually expects us to wear these tomorrow?" she told Pol. "Honestly!"

"What do you think you're doing!" Pol snapped angrily, sitting upright on the sofa and looking away from the girls. "Get back in your room and put something decent on!"

"Hey, it's not like we *want* to parade around like this," Maria said.

"I sure as hell hope not!"

Maria smirked. "You *are* getting to be just like Poppa!"

Blancanales realized how overprotective he was being and he brought himself under control. "Look, I just don't think these outfits are something you ought to be wearing around, okay?"

"That's what we tried telling Mae," Maria said. "Maybe she'd listen to you. . . ."

"I'll talk to her about it tomorrow. Promise," Pol said. "Now go change, would you?"

"Gladly."

Pol rose from the couch and went to the door of the trailer. He threw it open and looked out at the film set. Mae's Winnebago was across the way, a light on in one of the back windows. A single overhead halogen lamp lit the rest of the lot, casting long, eerie shadows, giving everything an aura of unreality. A gust of cold wind rushed into the trailer, and even after he'd closed the door Pol could still feel the chill hovering around him. Of all the members of Able Team, he considered himself the least prone to inklings about sixth senses or other paranormal occurrences, but somehow he couldn't get over the feeling that somewhere, somehow, things around here weren't quite right....

10

Lyons, Grimaldi and Schwarz were staying at Slumberama, a low-rent fantasy-theme motel a few miles west of Cincinnati. They had a room with wallpapered scenery showing the Bavarian Alps and a grand castle built by one of the mad kings who had ruled the land in days of yore. A plastic bird in an imitation Swiss Cuckoo clock had just come out to announce it was one in the morning when the phone next to Lyons's bed rang.

"Yeah?" Lyons blurted into the mouthpiece.

"I think we're on to something," Kurtzman told him. "Are you guys ready to move?"

"Hell, yes!" Lyons stretched one leg out and jarred Schwarz's bed to prevent his partner from falling asleep again. Gadgets threw off his covers and mouthed Kurtzman's name silently. When Lyons nodded affirmatively, Schwarz grabbed for his clothes and started dressing. Grimaldi was still snoring on a fold-out cot on the other side of the room. Schwarz had to call out his name three times before the aviator came to.

Aaron Kurtzman related the information he'd just culled from his computer scan of data being put out by all law enforcement agencies within a hundred-mile radius of Cincinnati. "Some stoolie in Napolean, Indiana, just got through talking to the state police. Says he overheard a couple guys at a truck stop talking up a big weapons shipment bound for Cincy. Fabyan's name came up in the conversation, so it's a safe bet we're talking mob guns.''

Lyons cradled the receiver between his chin and shoulder as he jerked open a drawer in the nightstand and pulled out some of the motel's complimentary stationary. "How long ago?" he asked, readying a pen to take notes.

"Not quite an hour. The guy waited till they left the stop so he could get a make on the truck," Kurtzman said. "It's a sixteen-wheeler. Says 'Bedford Quarries' on each side. Napoleon's about forty miles from the state line, so you can figure they're probably in Ohio by now."

Lyons scribbled his pen across the notepad. "Any ideas where in Cincy they're headed?"

"No, but there's an APB out on the truck. I'll stay patched into the highway patrol and reach you on the communicators once there's a sighting."

"Good," Lyons said. "We'll hit the road and hope we don't miss out."

"Any new word on Lao Ti?"

"Still holding her own," Lyons reported. "I'll check the hospital again once this is over."

"Good luck."

Lyons hung up and grabbed his keys off the nightstand. Schwarz was already dressed. Grimaldi moved slowly, as if he was underwater.

"Here," Lyons said, tossing the keys to Gadgets. "Get the car started. I'll be right behind you."

"You got it."

"Get it in gear, Jack," Lyons told Grimaldi as he threw on a shirt and pants.

Grimaldi yawned. "I think I liked things better when I was just a lowly fly-boy...."

BEDFORD QUARRIES WAS half owned by Peter "Gun" Cinzo, underboss of the Cleveland-based Cinzo family and one of the imprisoned mob figures looking at hard time as a result of Nash Felsur's grand jury testimony. It had only taken Dave X. Fabyan a quick phone call to the quarry boss to requisition the semis needed to clean out Eddie Nevrut's hoard of stolen Naval arms. One of the trucks was already up in New Stanton and the other, filled with the lion's share of the haul, was bound for one of Cinzo's Cincinnati cover establishments, a gravestone-manufacturing plant located next to a cemetery in Reading.

Two of Fabyan's soldiers, Vic Shepp and Rommie Carlucci, were handling the Cincy haul. Shepp was the archetypal heavy, six and a half feet tall and nearly three hundred pounds of Neanderthal brutality, while Carlucci was short, a flashy dresser with a pencil-thin mustache and more brains in his pinky than Shepp had between his huge jug ears. The big man was behind the wheel, eyes fixed on the highway before them. Carlucci was angry, and every few seconds he glanced at his dim-witted partner with a look of absolute loathing that had been festering inside him since they'd left the truck stop in Napoleon.

"I gotta put a friggin' muzzle on you, Shepp, is that it?"

"I'm tellin' ya, no one was listenin'," the driver insisted. "I ain't a complete idiot, you know."

"Says who?"

Shepp fumed silently, taking out his own anger on the plug of tobacco wedged between his teeth. He eased down on the accelerator and passed a slow-moving van in the right lane. When his cheeks had their fill of juice, he spat into a coffee tin hanging from the doorframe, then went back to his chewing. Working up his nerve, he finally told Carlucci, "You never answered my question, anyway."

The shorter man lit a cigarette and blew smoke against the truck's windshield. "What question?"

"What do you think they're gonna do with all these guns and shit?"

"Gee, I don't know, Shepp," Carlucci droned facetiously. "They'll probably give 'em back to the Navy and apologize for taking 'em in the first place."

That didn't make sense to Shepp. He bent his brow, thinking things through. "But the Navy place was just a few miles away from where we loaded up. If we were givin' 'em back—"

"Shit!" Carlucci swore, seeing the roof lights of a patrol car flash on in the rearview mirror.

"Oh, man!" Shepp moaned. "What do we do?"

Carlucci reached under the bench seat for an Ingram submachine gun. "Slow down and pull over. If that cop's lucky, he only caught us speeding."

11

Grimaldi was at the wheel of the Jeep, holding the vehicle at a steady fifty miles an hour in the westbound lane of the freeway. He stole sips from a cup of coffee between lane changes. Schwarz and Lyons had their eyes on traffic, looking for the truck.

"You guys wanna play Popeye?" Grimaldi asked.

"What?" Lyons said.

"You know, count cars with dead headlights. Two points for pickups and trucks, one for regular cars. Really makes the ol' time fly."

"Christ, Jack, I knew you weren't hitting on all cylinders, but this—"

"It was a *joke*, Ironman," Grimaldi interjected. "Look, guys, we gotta loosen up a little here, okay? Hell, the way we've been goin' since we got here, you'd think we'd been asked to fight the mob with one hand behind our back or something."

Lyons grinned at Schwarz as he told Grimaldi, "You keep being such a barrel of laughs, Jackster, and we're gonna lose you to the Carson show."

The three of them shared a much-needed laugh before the urgent blaring of Lyons's communicator sounded loudly in the Jeep.

"Yeah, Lyons here."

"Highway patrol just sighted the semi," Kurtzman called in. "Just passed the Taylors Creek junction, heading northeast on 275."

Lyons had already flashed on the cab light so he could refer to a fold-out map of Cincinnati. "Hot damn!" he exclaimed. "We're only a few miles away, heading west. H.P. making a stop?"

"Affirmative," Kurtzman reported. "Truck was speeding, so they're going to try to—"

"There!" Grimaldi interrupted, pointing across the freeway divider at the eastbound lane where two police cars had just parked behind an idling semi less than a quarter mile away.

"Later, Bear." Lyons signed off and put away the communicator in favor of his .45 Government Model Colt. "Can you get us over there, Jack?"

"I can sure as hell try," Grimaldi said, easing his way over to the far left lane and slowing down. Between the reinforced railings that separated east- and westbound lanes was a fifty-foot-wide gully. Even when he was able to squeeze the Jeep through a gap in the railing, Grimaldi still had doubts about getting to the eastbound lane, since nearly three feet of snow uniformly blanketed the no-man's-land between them and the semi. He forged headlong into the snow, which quickly came up past the underboy of the Jeep, bringing the vehicle to a halt. Shifting gears, he tried to back out, but they were stuck.

"So much for that plan," Grimaldi said, unbuckling his seat belt and pulling out his .45. "Looks like a nice night for a hike, eh, guys?"

The semi and two police cars were still a few hundred yards away. When the three men stepped out of the Jeep and promptly sank into snow up to their thighs, Lyons told Grimaldi, "Next time we'll just get off at an exit and take the bridge over, okay?"

"Pansy," Grimaldi needled.

HIGHWAY PATROL OFFICERS ROBERTS AND JONES got out of the first squad car, police revolvers in their hands. They approached the semi cautiously, forewarned that the occupants of the vehicle were likely to be armed and dangerous. When the second cruiser stopped on the shoulder moments later, Roberts whispered to his partner, "Thank God for a little backup."

They lingered near the back of the semi, waiting for support.

"Hold on," a tall uniformed man called out to his fellow officers as he stepped out of the passenger side of the second car. The driver, shorter and stockier, joined him moments later, and they walked together up to the first men on the scene.

"We just got word this is a false alarm," the driver reported, raising his voice to be heard above the few cars on the road at this hour of night.

"Say what?" Officer Jones muttered.

"Yeah," the tall man explained. "The semi we're really looking for was just nabbed up near Fairfield."

Roberts narrowed his eyes suspiciously. "How come we didn't get a call on that?"

"Like I said, we just got word," the other driver insisted. "Look, we heard you report these guys as speeding, so just ticket 'em and that'll be it."

Officer Roberts was still unconvinced. Both he and Jones kept their guns out. "You guys are east-side," he said, noting the badge number of the tall man. "How'd you get here so fast, anyway?"

Before the tall man could respond, a third vehicle, this one an unmarked sedan, swerved off the highway and screeched to a halt at an angle in front of the semi, blocking its path. Two uniformed U.S. Marshals bolted out of the passenger's side. One aimed up at Carlucci and Shepp inside the semi while the other pointed his revolver at the cops standing next to Roberts and Jones.

"Freeze!"

Abe Abko got out from behind the wheel of the sedan, adding his gun to the display of firepower.

"Jig's up, boys," he shouted at the east-side cops. "We know whose pocket you're in, so don't waste your breath on fairy tales."

"FLOOR IT and let's get outta here!" Remmie Carlucci snapped at Vic Shepp inside the semi.

"But that car—"

"Run the goddamn thing over if you have to! Just hit it!"

Carlucci had already rolled down his window. In one smooth, ferretlike motion, he sprang upward, pushing off the bench seat and out the window so he could fire his Ingram over the cab's roof. His first bursts took out the marshal who'd been aiming at him.

Shepp had swallowed his tobacco in his fear, and he was choking for breath as he jammed the truck's gears and pulled forward, bearing down on Abko's sedan. A bullet shattered the window next to him and was deflected enough by the impact that it pierced his throat at an angle, making a mess of his jugular vein and windpipe. Shepp slumped over the wheel, already dead, but his foot stayed on the semi's accelerator.

ABKO HAD LITTLE TIME to admire his first shot. The monstrous truck slammed into his car, and he had to throw himself sharply to the pavement to avoid being crushed under the front end as it swung around toward him. The move brought him out into view of Carlucci, who had yet to realize that Shepp was no longer at control behind the wheel.

The short mobster burped his Ingram, stitching the pavement in a tight zigzag pattern.

"Goddamn!" Abko swore as the .45 ACP rounds pounded into him.

The taller of the east-side cops had his gun out before his partner, and he killed both Jones and Roberts at point-blank range. He wasn't sure how the fat guy in the other car had found out about his mob connections, but the tall man wasn't going to stick around to ask questions. Ducking the same hail of shots that brought down his partner, he scrambled back to their squad car. As he reached for the door, however, a spray of gunfire scarred the metal, forcing him away. He glanced over his shoulder and saw three gunmen wading toward him through the snow separating the lanes of the highway.

"Maybe you should stick around," Lyons advised, pulling himself up out of the drift and shaking loose snow from his legs. Grimaldi and Schwarz were right behind him, and when the tall man slipped inside the squad car and prepared to make a run for it, they cut loose with enough ammunition to chew through the car door. The tall man sat still in the wake of the gunshots. Then his body tipped to one side, pushing the door open. He fell to the ground, blood on his uniform.

Lyons's attention turned to the semi, which skidded down the highway only a few dozen yards before jackknifing out of control. Remmie Carlucci was thrown clear of the cab window and landed on his back on the asphalt seconds before the truck's payload toppled onto its side, blocking all five lanes of the highway and crushing the diminutive gunsel underneath several tons of misshapen metal and contraband weaponry.

Traffic slowly began to back up west of the war zone. Lyons, Grimaldi and Schwarz strode past the squad cars and the bodies of the slain police officers to where the one unharmed U.S. Marshal was crouching over the bleeding form of Abe Abko. The burly man was still alive, and when he looked up and saw Lyons standing over him, he gloated weakly, ''Okay, fucker. About that apology...''

12

With filming slated to begin within the hour, the last thing
Claudette and Otto wanted to contend with was an uprising
by their technical advisor. But Pol Blancanales was ada-
mant. Interrupting the production team's hectic breakfast
near one of the propane heaters next to Claudette's Winnebago, Pol, flanked by his sister and Veronica Rammite, is-
sued his ultimatum. Unless the girls were allowed to wear
less suggestive outfits during the opening shot, he would
refuse to lend any last-minute support staging the difficult
climactic scene.

Blancanales had expected to have a fight on his hands, but
Otto and Claudette merely exchanged glances over their
cups of coffee and reached a surprising consensus.

"Okay, no problem," Claudette said. She turned to Bendellan. "Otto, be a dear and take the girls to the wardrobe
truck and see if we have anything else they might feel more
comfortable in."

"Sure thing," Otto replied, equally unperturbed. He got
up from the director's chair by the heater and pointed to one
of the trailers in the background, telling Maria and Veronica, "Come along...."

Blancanales stayed behind, slipping into the seat Otto had
abandoned. "I don't get it," he muttered.

"Get what?" Claudette asked, dividing her attention between Pol, her notes and a hard buttered roll that was her
breakfast.

"You gave in so easy...."

Claudette tilted her head back slightly and laughed, "I guess I did, didn't I? Well, in this business you have to learn to choose your battles carefully. In this case, I don't think what those girls wear is going to make or break the film. However, your department's another story."

"Well, I think everything's all set on that front," Pol said. "The weapons come in yet?"

Claudette nodded. She took one last bite of her roll and stood up. "They're inside," she said, starting up the steps to her Winnebago. "Come and have a look."

Pol followed the woman into the mobile home. Half the main room was taken up by opened crates filled with the various guns, grenades and rifles Blancanales had ordered for the siege scene. He marveled at the collection, picking up and looking over several of the items.

"This stuff is all cherry," he remarked. "Mae, how'd you get your hands on guns that have never even been fired?"

"Trade secret," Claudette replied with a wink. "But it has something to do with free advertising."

"Like all the times you see people drinking Coke or Pepsi in the movies?" Pol guessed.

"Yeah, that's the idea. Of course, people aren't going to be able to walk out of the theater and buy themselves a Colt Commando at the local 7-11, but you get the idea."

A kettle on the stove began to whistle. Claudette went over and turned down the flame, then tossed a few tea bags into a quart thermos. "Fuel for the long haul," she explained to Pol as she added the boiling water.

"We better get cracking, huh?"

"In a minute." Claudette screwed the cap on the thermos, then moved close to Pol, looking into his eyes. She put her arms around his waist and pulled him nearer. Pol offered no resistance. When she rose slightly on tiptoe and moved her lips toward his, Pol closed his eyes and kissed her, feeling their mutual passion run through him even as he felt her quiver in his arms from the same tumultuous force. The embrace lasted only a few seconds, but when it was over Pol felt as if the moment had lingered on far longer, taking into account all those random fantasies he'd had about her the past two days.

"That should hold me until the end of shooting." She used her thumb to wipe lipstick from Pol's face. Their eyes met again. "Maybe then we can pick up where we left off."

"That would be nice," Pol had to admit.

"But now we have a small war to wage."

Claudette lapsed back into her more professional persona, tucking the thermos under her arm so that she had her hands free to hold a clipboard with filming instructions and the battery-operated bullhorn she planned to use when she was directing her cast through its well-rehearsed paces.

The film's Delta Force was outfitted in khaki and camouflage when Pol and Claudette emerged from the Winnebago. Blancanales started passing out the weapons and reminding the men of the special quirks they would have to take into consideration when using each item. There was something about the men that struck him as peculiar, and he was finally able to pinpoint it.

"How come you guys are all wearing gloves?" he asked Jimbo as he handed the big man one of the Colt Commandos.

"So our hands don't freeze," Jimbo replied quickly. "It may look warm out with that sun shining, but don't kid yourself."

"Maybe so, but there's no way Delta Force would wear gloves on an operation like this," Pol insisted. "No matter how snug they fit, you lose too much precision."

Jimbo glanced questioningly at Claudette, who intervened on the men's behalf. "I really don't think an audience is going to be paying that much attention to whether or not the men are wearing gloves, Pol. Let's let them keep warm, okay?''

Pol wanted to protest further, but caught himself. Hollywood logic strikes again, he thought privately. No sense making a scene at this point. What was it Mae had just told him? Know when to choose your battles. "Okay," he relented. "Gloves it is."

WITH THE VIXENISH APLOMB of femme fatales out of an old forties movie, Maria and Veronica sashayed past the brownfaced pseudo-Iranian guards, wearing calf-length fake fur coats and high leather boots with spiked heels. Batting their thick false eyelashes, the young women paused before the gateway to the old depot and asked the guards to light their cigarettes. The diversion went off flawlessly.

Sam was working one camera up close to the depot while Claudette had another trained on Rudy, Jimbo and the other would-be Delta Force marauders. Pol stood behind Claudette, using hand signals to cue the men through the intricate maneuvers as they staged their assault on the supposedly impregnable Iranian fortress. They shot four takes over three hours.

There was little dialogue to bother with. Timing was the primary concern, and Otto roamed the set constantly like a worrisome coach, a stopwatch in one hand, a still camera in the other. Special-effects charges had been set throughout the set to simulate gunfire and even grenade blasts, and theatrical blood flowed from cosmetic wounds during strategic parts of the shooting.

Pol was amazed by their professionalism, admiring the proficiency of Mae's lean crew and conceding the credibility of most of the action stunts surrounding the raid of the compound, the killing of the guards and the escape using prop explosives. If the script was to be believed, the wall of fire that resulted from the explosives could easily have ignited the charges and blown the heroes to oblivion and back. The biggest difference between the staged action and Pol's actual experience in similar situations was the noise level. In life, Pol knew, a raid of this magnitude would create such a persistent, cumulative din that his ears would ring for days after the bombing and gunshots had ceased. On the set the "grenades" gave off smoke and simulated shrapnel in relative silence, and the crackle of gunfire was even less obtrusive than some cap-pistol wars he remembered from his childhood. Most of the sound would be dubbed in later, Mae explained to him during a short break between takes. That way, they didn't have to worry about extraneous noises on the set during shooting. The lower noise level also kept down the number of curiosity-seekers dropping by to gawk at the proceedings.

"Cut!" Claudette stepped away from her camera and gave the assembled cast and crew a triumphant thumbs-up signal. "That's a wrap!"

There was a spontaneous burst of cheers and applause on the set. It was late afternoon, and everyone was exhausted from the grueling pace they'd kept up throughout the day. The vending van returned with a specially requested supply of prepared meals, and people took refuge inside the old depot, where tables and chairs were already set up. The celebratory mood lasted through dinner and into the early hours of evening, when darkness brought with it a new cold front and the prospect of more snow.

The group inside the depot gradually dwindled, until only a handful of diehards remained at one of the tables.

"When do you think we'll be able to see the rushes?" Maria asked Claudette.

"Oh, sometime tomorrow morning, before you have to catch your flight back to Los Angeles."

Veronica groaned with disappointment. "This all went too fast. It seems like we just got here."

"Maybe it seems that way to you," Claudette chuckled, "but I feel like it's been forever."

"Well, I guess we should get back to the trailer and start packing," Maria told Veronica. She stifled a yawn. "If I don't get a better night's sleep, I'm going to doze off during the dailies tomorrow."

"I'll be there in a bit," Pol told the girls.

Otto excused himself as well, leaving Blancanales alone with Claudette. The woman nibbled the last of her carrot cake, pretending not to notice Pol's eyes on her.

"Well . . ." he finally prompted her, "the war's over."

"Indeed." Claudette wiped her lips with a napkin, then rose from her chair. "Come on, let's have a nightcap."

"Your place or mine?" Pol wisecracked.

"I think we'll have a little more privacy at mine, don't you?"

Pol grinned. "A woman after my own heart."

Claudette let her gaze drift down Pol's muscular body. "I had something a little lower in mind, actually."

THE LIQUOR CABINET in Claudette's Winnebago was well stocked, but Pol decided to stick with beer. He uncapped a Heineken and nonchalantly pulled aside the curtain that blocked off the driver's seat from the living quarters of the mobile home. Outside, he could see the work crew diligently stripping the set under the glow of the halogen lamp.

"You really think they'll finish all that tonight?" he asked.

"Of course," Claudette said, nuzzling up close to Pol. "For what we're paying them, you better believe they will. And I think they can do it without our supervision, Pol."

She took him by the hand and led him back into the main room. He was forced to set down his beer as she drew him into another tight, lingering embrace. Up until then, Pol had been having second thoughts about consummating their relationship, figuring that a few days from now they would be off in their own worlds, unlikely ever to connect again. Now, however, with her in his arms, the fact that they would be going their own separate ways seemed to make a bout of frenzied lovemaking even more appealing. A bit of passion with no strings attached might not be a bad thing, he mused.

"Before we get too carried away," Claudette whispered in his ear once they broke their kiss to come up for air, "how about doing me a quick favor by finding some nice music, hmmmm?"

"Okay." Pol kissed her again, then moved over to the stereo console and began sorting through stacks of cassettes. His back was turned, giving Claudette her chance to remove a small glass vial from inside her bra. There was a clear liquid inside the container, and she quickly emptied it into the bottle of Heineken.

Pol chose a jazz tape and filled the Winnebago with the lush, sensual sounds of a soprano saxophone. Claudette bobbed her head in time with the music and swayed slowly from side to side, sipping her gin and tonic. Pol took a long swallow of beer, then held his arms out, inviting Claudette to dance. She obliged.

"Oh, you're quite the dancer," she murmured huskily, pressing herself close to Blancanales, letting him feel the supple curves of her body.

"I've cut a few rugs," Pol admitted, neatly dipping the woman to one side and then swinging her up again. The scent of her perfume rose up toward him, intoxicating in its subtlety.

Less subtle was the impact of his spiked drink. One second he was just beginning to notice a certain light-headedness, the next his knees gave out and he fell away from the woman, landing hard on the carpeted floor, his mind at the mercy of a pharmaceutical pied piper called propranolol.

"Pleasant dreams, silly boy," Claudette whispered.

13

In mid-1944, a pivotal period of World War II, British Prime Minister Winston Churchill became so incensed over Germany's persistent V-1 bombings of his country that he pushed for ways to hit the Nazis back and hit them hard. Although the Allies were gaining the upper hand, it looked as if the war on the European front was destined to drag on interminably unless some means was applied to force a surrender. Of course, the Manhattan Project was in high gear, readying the atomic bomb, but Western leaders, and particularly Churchill, didn't want to place their sole hopes on a nuclear solution. There had to be other ways.

One of the options considered was the use of anthrax bombs. Anthrax, a lethally contagious disease triggered by contact with the microbe Bacillus anthracis, had hideous potential in terms of military applications. Allied intelligence forces had caught wind that Japan had resorted to the use of anthrax against China in isolated areas of the Asian mainland with devastating results. Although such use clearly violated the 1925 Geneva Convention, which both Britain and the United States had signed, the course of the war and the deadly stakes prompted Churchill to consider expediency in the name of the greater good and press for an anthrax solution.

President Roosevelt was adamantly opposed to any form of biochemical warfare, but with the Axis powers showing few signs of losing strength in the foreseeable future, the

U.S. reluctantly became a party to development of a highly confidential strategy for the use of anthrax bombs. At the Midwest Research Center, a remote high-security plant in Vigo County, near Terre Haute, Indiana, a breakneck-paced schedule was handed down, calling for the production of fifty thousand bombs by the summer of 1944 and a quarter million of the weapons by the end of the year.

For a variety of reasons, foremost among them being unrealistic expectations by those who placed the initial order, American production at the Indiana plant fell behind schedule from the outset and an adequate supply of the anthrax bombs never materialized. More conventional battle strategies, particularly the D-Day invasion of Normandy and Russia's drive to expel Nazi troops from the Soviet homeland, succeeded in striking a decisive blow against the enemy, and by the end of 1945 Allied victory seemed close at hand.

When the Indiana anthrax project was subsequently scrapped, most of the bombs that had already been created were transferred to the nearby Newport Army Ammunition Plant. However, a small stockpile of the weapons remained behind at the Midwest Research Center, which continued to receive government funding for clandestine research into biochemical weapons. With the primary focus gradually shifting toward the creation of binary chemical munitions, in which separated, nonlethal components are combined to undergo their deadly transformation only when a warhead is en route to its intended target, the anthrax stockpile fell by the wayside. Plans were made for the removal of the bombs, now deemed to be obsolete at best and highly unstable at worse, but due to routine bureaucratic foot-dragging and budgetary considerations, the weapons remained at both Newport and the research plant.

By no small coincidence, the Midwest Research Center was located less than fifty miles away from New Stanton,

Indiana. Furthermore, the layout of the research plant and its storage facility for the anthrax bombs had been exactly duplicated as the set for Claudette Simms's supposed filming of *You Ran, Iran*. Unknown to Pol Blancanales, his sister and Veronica Rammite, there had been no film in the cameras shooting their cinematic debuts. What they considered to be the final take had only been a dress rehearsal.

THAT NIGHT, at precisely 11:03 p.m., Claudette Simms slowed a 1983 Chevy Impala to a sputtering halt less than twenty feet away from the main gate to the research center. Pretending to be drunk and flustered, she staggered out of the car, her blouse half-unbuttoned beneath her short fur coat. A black miniskirt hiked its way up her long legs when she walked. Raising the hood of the car, she leaned over to inspect the engine, providing the guards in front of the main entrance with a more-than-fleeting glimpse up her legs. When the men masked their lust with chivalry and came to offer assistance, Jimbo, Rudy and the other Blancanales-trained commandos crept out of the surrounding darkness and gave the performances of their lives.

The raid on the compound was carried out with calculated precision, and less than fifteen minutes after it had begun, the siege was over. Twelve employees of Midwest Research, ten of them security guards, lay dead, whereas the intruders had suffered only one fatality. Isolated as the plant was, there was no immediate intervention by anyone attracted by the gunfire. The facility's alarm system had been neutralized during the initial phase of the attack, and therefore it would be some time before authorities learned what had happened.

One dozen anthrax bombs were carefully transferred to one of the film trailers parked several hundred yards away and then driven to a nearby clearing along the Wabash

River, where a second transfer was made to a waiting Bell UH-1H Iroquois helicopter.

Half of the commando squad climbed aboard the chopper to accompany the bombs on their flight to Wyoming. Claudette ran over and got into a waiting limousine, sharing the front seat with Dave X. Fabyan and Otto Bendellan. Maria Blancanales and Veronica Rammite were bound and gagged in the back seat, still unconscious from doses of the same knock-out drug Claudette had used on Pol.

"Looks like things have gone right for a change," Fabyan commented as he watched the Bell lift off.

"Let's get out of here," Claudette told Otto, who was at the wheel. "We can brag once we're on that jet and heading back to the ranch."

Rudy and Jimbo remained behind to tidy up one last bit of unfinished business. They dragged the slain raider across the snow to where Claudette's Winnebago had been parked behind some shrubs. Pol Blancanales was strapped in behind the steering wheel, still unconscious. The dead man was placed in the passenger seat before Jimbo started up the mobile home's engine. Putting the vehicle into gear, Jimbo slipped out and walked alongside, keeping one hand on the steering wheel so that he could guide the Winnebago's course. Once they came to a steep incline that led down to the Wabash River, Jimbo placed Blancanales's right foot on the accelerator, then jumped clear.

Picking up speed, the Winnebago charged down the hill, jumping clear of the road and crashing through a wooden fence before plummeting over a pitched embankment and splashing loudly into the icy current. For a brief moment, the vehicle bobbed on the surface, but as water seeped in it began to list to one side and slowly sink.

14

Cold. Wet. Pain. Air. Like kites in a fog, words and sensations flitted through Pol Blancanales's brain.

Sleep. Peaceful. Sleeping pills. Mae.

Snippets of memory came back to him, strings to reel the kites in with.

Mae put me to sleep. A trick. Danger, Pol. Beware.

The submerged Winnebago shifted with the river's current, jostling Blancanales.

Wake up!

He opened his eyes. Darkness. Wet, cold. I'm in water. Can't move. Numb. Seat belt. He was strapped in on his side. Water was creeping up past his chest, lapping against his chin. There was something underneath him, trying to float to the surface. Brushing against him.

A body!

"No!" Pol shouted. "Noooooo!"

He breathed greedily, then closed his mouth and leaned his head below the waterline for a moment. When he came back up for air, shaking water from his face, he was fully conscious, free of the drug.

Be calm. Don't panic. Think things through.

He was in the Winnebago. It was underwater, tipped on its side. He was strapped in the driver's seat, up above the waterline. Even if the vehicle was completely submerged, he knew there would still be a pocket of air to sustain him temporarily.

Clawing at the seat belt, he found the buckle and un-snapped it, freeing himself from the seat. By lowering his feet to the passenger door beneath him, he could stand.

There was still no light.

The body nudged him again. He grabbed a wrist. No pulse. He pushed the corpse away.

Cold. The water was freezing. He had to get out before his body temperature fell any further.

The driver's door was overhead, but the water exerted too much pressure on the door for him to open it. With the water up to his chin, he couldn't muster enough strength to break the windshield, either.

The window. He grabbed the crank handle hard and leaned his full weight into turning it. The window slowly began to lower, letting more water surge in. Pol filled his lungs with air and continued rolling the window down, holding his breath once he found himself completely sub-merged. Finally he was able to wriggle his way up through the opening.

Exhaling slowly, he curled over so he could untie his boots, then squirmed out of his coat and floated upward, feeling his lungs beg and burn for more air.

When he reached the surface, Pol gasped, treading wa-ter, orienting himself. The river pulled him along with its gentle current as he tried to swim toward shore. In his weakened condition, however, the short distance seemed hopelessly unreachable.

By a stroke of good fortune, the river dragged him to a shallow bend, and when he couldn't swim any farther, Pol lowered his legs and found he could touch bottom. Tread-ing through the murky sediment, he felt the mud suck at his feet with each step as if trying to pull him under again. His legs began to go numb from the cold. Finally, though, he managed to reach the embankment and pull himself from the water. Rolling over on his back, he looked up at the cloud-choked sky. Off in the distance he could hear traffic slowing to a halt, then the slamming of car doors and the sound of feet trampling snow as they drew closer to him. Before he could discover who was coming, however, Pol slipped back into the black void.

HE WOKE UP IN A HOSPITAL BED. The room around him was white and warm in contrast to the darkness and coldness of the sunken Winnebago. The chill was gone from his bones, and a quick flex test confirmed that he still had use of his extremities. He was sore, hungry and tired as hell, and his brain still felt as if it were clogged with cotton candy, but shit, it was good to be alive.

Before Pol had a chance to get carried away with euphoria, he noticed that he wasn't alone in the room.

A tall nurse stood beside his bed, changing one of the suspended bottles dripping fluids through clear tubes into his veins. She noticed that he'd come to, and the look she gave him was one of barely concealed disdain.

"Was it something I said?" he inquired with a smirk.

"Just stay put," the nurse told him. "The police have been waiting to speak with you."

"Good."

The nurse slipped out of the room. From where he was lying, Pol could see out the window. It looked like mid-morning outside. He started to sit up for a better view and realized that he was handcuffed to his bed.

"What the hell?" he mumbled.

The door to his room swung open and two men in lined trench coats strode to his bedside. The taller man was pale and jowly, with thin eyebrows arched in a constant expression of annoyance. His hair was even thinner, slicked back on his head in a strange swirl that attempted to cover a prominent bald spot. He flashed a badge and introduced himself as Lieutenant Lanski.

"And this is Officer Jensen," Lanski said, gesturing toward the trim, square-jawed black man who pulled up a seat at the foot of Pol's bed and stared at the patient through round wire-rimmed glasses. "He's the one that found you."

"I appreciate that," Pol said. He tugged at his handcuffs, drawing the cops' attention to them. "These really aren't necessary."

"We'll be the judge of that," Lanski said.

Pol eased back in the bed. "I don't get it."

"You're under arrest," Jensen informed him.

"What?"

"You have the right to remain silent," Lanski intoned, reciting Miranda from memory. "Anything you say can and will be used against you in a court of law. You have the right to an attorney. If you can't afford—"

"I know my rights, okay?" Pol said. "What's the charge?"

Lanski chortled sardonically. "Mr. Blancanales, we've got you on more charges than Baskin-Robbins has flavors. Start at murder and work your way down to grand theft auto and—"

"Murder?" Pol exclaimed. "Grand theft? What the hell are you talking about? Look, one minute I was dancing with this lady after a film shoot, and the next thing I knew I was drowning at the bottom of some river!"

"Amnesia?" Lanski said. "That it? Or maybe you want to push your luck and go for temporary insanity, hmmm?"

Pol looked up at the ceiling as if seeking heavenly intervention. "Look, I don't know what's happened, but I've been framed."

"Oh, framed now?" Lanski looked at his associate. "This guy can't make up his mind, Jensen? How about if we help him out?"

The black man pulled a small notebook from his trench coat and licked his thumb before slipping to a page filled with handwriting only he could ever have hoped to read. "Your name is Rosario Blancanales. You've spent most of your life in the military, but there are a lot of gaps in your record over the past few years. Our guess is you were playing mercenary then—probably in Angola, maybe Central America."

"Wrong," Pol protested.

Jensen went on as if Blancanales hadn't spoken. "We figure you and some of your buddies put together a little hit team and decided to go into business for yourselves. Knocked over a little research center outside of Terre Haute and made off with some poison bombs."

"What?"

"Shut up, I'm not finished," Jensen snapped. He went back to his notes and briefly described the siege on the plant, which Pol quickly realized was a clone operation of the depot assault he'd spent so much time plotting for Mae Jung and her film crew...or whoever they were.

"You must have been in too much of a hurry on the getaway," Jensen continued, "and you ended up in the drink along with one of your cronies who didn't fare so well. The rest of your buddies kept on going. How's that for starters?"

Pol shook his head. "You put two and two together and got twenty-two when the right answer's four."

"I don't think so," Lanski countered. "We fished out your little Winnebago and found all kinds of goodies with your name on 'em. Registration slips, contracts, the works. Quite an operation you set up, I gotta say."

Pol fell silent a moment, trying to put the picture into focus. Working from the premise that he'd let himself be played for a prize chump by whoever Mae Jung really was, things were starting to make sense. While he thought he'd been playing an innocent game of Mr. Hollywood, he'd really been hired to mastermind this munitions heist the cops were talking about. The more he put it together, the more he almost felt as if he deserved to take the rap for whatever might have happened. How could you be such an idiot, Blancanales? Blinded by a pretty face and some easy money, like some half-wit.

Remembering how the "Delta Force" had worn gloves the entire day of shooting, he told Jensen, "Let me guess. You found some weapons, and the only fingerprints on 'em were mine."

Jensen smiled, not pleasantly. "Whaddaya know! The man's got his memory back."

The image of his sister and Veronica Rammite flashed through Pol's mind, and an icy chill snaked down his spine. "And you haven't found any of the others?" he asked the cops.

Lanski rolled his shoulders and ran his hand over his head, pressing the loose hairs down over his bald spot. "Not yet, but you're going to help us out with that, aren't you?"

"I sure as hell am," Pol said determinedly, "but not the way you think. I want to make my phone call now, if you don't mind."

Jensen got up from his chair and grabbed a telephone off the nightstand next to Pol's bed. He handed it over to Blancanales, who hurriedly took the receiver and stabbed his fingers at the touch-tone numbers. He wasn't about to waste his time on lawyers. The call he put through was to Stony Man Farm.

15

Hal Brognola had already deplaned at Greater Cincinnati Airport and made his way to the terminal gateway by the time Jack Grimaldi and Gadgets Schwarz arrived to greet him.

"Traffic," Grimaldi offered as their excuse for being late.

"No problem." Brognola turned up the collar of his overcoat against the cold draft blowing in through an opened doorway. He carried an overnight bag and a brief-case, but from his haggard expression one might have guessed he was also carrying the burdens of all mankind on his shoulders.

"So what's all this about Pol?" Schwarz asked as the three men exited the terminal and got into the Jeep.

Brognola related his conversation with Blancanales as they headed out of the airport and linked up with the 175 for the trip back to Cincinnati. Contrary to its name, the airport was actually in Kentucky, and they had to cross the Ohio River near Covington before actually reentering the Cincinnati city limits. The Stony Man leader had also brought along some additional information he and Kurtz-man had tracked down following Pol's call.

"What a damn mess!" Schwarz muttered after Brognola had brought things up to date.

"That'll teach him to try moonlighting on us," Grimaldi said. The wisecrack failed to dent their somber mood, and the traffic's snail pace played further on the men's nerves.

"As it turns out," Brognola said, "without realizing it, Pol was working on the same general mission as you guys."

"Huh? You want to run that by again?" Grimaldi put on the brakes as the cars ahead of him came to a halt halfway across the bridge linking Ohio and Kentucky. Up ahead they could see the huge edifice of Riverfront Stadium, where football fans leaving a charity exhibition game between the Bengals and a college all-star team were contributing to the congestion on the streets.

"Kurtzman ran a check on the ordnance you guys helped nab off that semi last night," Brognola explained. "The same kind of weapons were used on the heist in Terre Haute, it turns out. Same sequence of serial numbers in some cases."

"Incredible," Schwarz mumbled. "Goddamn mob has its fingers in everything around here."

"You really aren't that surprised, are you?" Brognola asked him.

"No, not really."

"What I don't get," Grimaldi said, "is what the hell the syndicate would want with a bunch of outdated bombs."

"Simple," Brognola told him, chomping on one of his cigars. "It was a theft waiting to happen. That center had weaker security than any other depot in the country."

Traffic picked up. Grimaldi ventured over to the far right lane and got off at the hospital exit. "Why the hell wasn't the place better guarded?" he asked the chief.

"Hell, I'm sure some commission will look into it and come up with a few dozen reasons," Brognola predicted. "Lax procedures, budget cuts, guys out sick . . . you name it."

"They probably figured that since the stockpile was supposed to be top secret they'd be better off not drawing attention to it," Schwarz speculated.

"At any rate, it's done, and they're out there somewhere plotting their next move."

Grimaldi drove into the parking garage next to the hospital and found a spot on the second level. As he turned off the ignition, he wondered aloud, "Just what kind of damage can they do with those bombs?"

Brognola stepped out of the Jeep and, after a chew, dropped his cigar and crushed it under his foot. It was a dramatic gesture, effectively impressing Grimaldi and Schwarz with the gravity of what he was about to say.

"They have a dozen missiles, each one of them filled with 106 separate four-pound bombs. From all the data we have, that's a potent enough dose to destroy life over an area of three square miles."

"APOLOGY ACCEPTED," Abe Abko said from his hospital bed. He stuck out a beefy hand and added, "Pay the cleaners for getting the guacamole outta my suit and we're even."

Carl Lyons leaned forward and shook the marshal's hand, telling him, "Fair enough. How you doing, anyway?"

Abko pulled up his hospital gown and revealed the fresh round scars left by .45 bullets and the surgery required to pull them out of his right side. "Holier than thou," he snorted.

Lyons cracked a smile and pulled a chair up next to his onetime nemesis. "So tell me, how'd you finger those guys who were on the take?" he asked. "Hell, they aren't even on your force."

"For a loudmouth jerk, I got a lotta friends in this burg," Abko bragged. "After our little dance at Dawn Juan's I got to thinking maybe I *could* figure out who blabbed the transfer change. I called in a few favors at Internal Affairs and got a sheet on people suspected of being too chummy with Fabyan. Two names jumped out at me, and damn if they weren't partners. They'd just gone on duty when I put out the APB about you bringing Felsur in by way of Hamstead, so I figured they were our boys.''

"Regular Sherlock, aren't you?" Lyons said.

Abko laughed, "Naw. If I had any brains I would have wasted that weasel with the Ingram first instead of his partner. Goddamn .45 slugs, anyway. You know they told me it'll be six weeks before my gut'll be able to handle solid foods?''

"Good chance to get rid of some of that extra insulation," Lyons told the marshal, glancing at Abko's ample midsection.

"Maybe I'll write a book," Abko groaned. *"The Gunshot Diet."*

"Look, Abe," Carl said. "I don't want to drag you back to business, but we're in a bind with this whole Fabyan bit. You heard about his guys raiding a bomb plant in Terre Haute?''

Abko nodded and pointed at the television hanging from the ceiling in the corner of his room. "Film at eleven.''

"What do you figure they'll do with the bombs?''

"You really gotta ask?''

"I guess not," Lyons said. "They'll want Cinzo and the other family heads set free, right?''

"That's what they'll start with, probably." Abko winced as he shifted his position on the bed. Before he could resume, an intercom speaker over the doorway broke through with an urgent message.

"Code blue, ICU.''

Lyons had been to enough hospitals to know what was happening. Someone in intensive care had just lost their vital signs.

Lao Ti.

"Look, I gotta go," Lyons told the marshal, rising from his chair. "Take care, hear?''

"Sneak me a Twinkie next time you come by," Abko requested, but Lyons was already out of the room.

At the intensive care unit, Lyons was stopped by an insistent orderly at the nursing station.

"No visitors right now," the orderly said.

From the station, Lyons was able to see teams of nurses and physicians swarming into Lao Ti's room. Two doctors were already poised on either side of her bed, ready to apply electric defibrilators on her chest in hopes of jump-starting her heart.

"Hang tough, lady," Lyons called out to her. As he backtracked to the adjacent waiting room, he met up with Schwarz, Grimaldi and Brognola.

"She the one that coded?" the chief asked.

Lyons nodded.

"Hell."

The men fell silent and took seats around a vacant table near the doorway. Off in the background, a situation comedy blared on another television. There was plenty of canned laughter, but no one in the room was in a mood to join in. Six agonizing minutes passed.

The same officious voice came over the speaker. "Cancel code blue."

Lyons leaned to one side and was able to see Lao Ti's room. The doctors and nurses were slowly filing out. Two orderlies wheeled out the defibrilator unit. Next to Lao Ti's bed, the cardiograph monitor had been left on. It was registering a pulse.

"Yes!" Lyons whispered encouragingly.

16

In 1944, Kenneth Shanks, a twenty-two-year-old whiz kid out of Ohio State's biochemistry program, was lured into the forefront of the anthrax bomb program at the Midwest Research Center. The program's failure to mass-produce weapons for use against the Germans was not Shanks's fault. If anything, his prodigious talents and stalwart dedication were responsible for overcoming numerous technical obstacles in the complicated planning stages of the operation. It came as little surprise to those who knew of his contributions that following the war he was asked to stay on at the Terre Haute facility as head of their research program.

Over the next thirty years he devoted himself to his job, becoming one of the Defense Department's key answer men on the subject of biological warfare strategies. He served on the cutting edge of this highly sensitive, highly classified venture, overseeing some of the major developments in gene-splicing and the creation of antiviral vaccines.

His stature in the scientific community for most of that period was untarnished and unquestioned, but by the mid-seventies, as computerized high-tech methods of research became the vanguard, Shanks had become too entrenched in his long-held ways to remain in step with modernization. He bristled at suggestions that bright up-and-coming scientists out of MIT, Cal Poly and Stanford should be brought into Midwest Research to help the facility keep up with the times. For some time he was able to back his obstinacy by putting in extra hours and continuing to uphold his reputation. But when the eighties rolled around and a new administration took over the White House, Shanks saw his budget at Midwest stagnating while heftier, more prestigious contracts were going to schools and research centers catering to what he called the "Young Jerks."

Two years ago, Midwest Research changed owners and the new board of directors called Shanks on the carpet, demanding drastic changes in the way things were run at the facility. The embittered scientist, never known for his tact, lashed back at the board with a raging diatribe about how he was being persecuted by lesser, envious minds. The board was of a different opinion, however, and Shanks was fired on the spot for insubordination.

Deprived of his livelihood—in fact the only life he knew— Shanks floundered through the next two years, for the most part staying inside his cramped Terre Haute apartment, writing abusive letters to his former employer, to the Defense Department and to all the other imagined tormentors he held responsible for what he considered to be a forced exile.

When he finally did get out of the house, it was to sate his more basic appetites. Over the years he had saved a considerable amount of money by virtue of his Spartan lifestyle, but during an eight-month period of unchecked self-indulgence, Shanks blew his entire savings on alcohol, prostitutes and gambling. A lot of his money eventually ended up in the hands of Dave X. Fabyan and the Cinzo family. When one of the call girls working for Fabyan's organization came forward with word about a half-crazed lecher who'd recently been involved with top-secret weapons research, the syndicate *capo* tracked down Shanks and befriended the man, building up his ravaged ego and giving him an opportunity to once again feel important.

It was Shanks who provided Fabyan and Claudette Simms with the information needed to plan the anthrax heist at Midwest Research Center, and when the Bell UH-1H chopper arrived at Simms's Wyoming ranch the morning after that theft, the sixty-six-year-old scientist was part of the welcoming committee.

Under Shanks's supervision, the deadly bombs were carefully transferred from the Bell's cargo hold to the larger of the two film processing labs inside the converted barn. In accordance with the scientist's specifications, the processing equipment had been removed and replaced by materials needed for the assignment he'd spent the past months preparing for.

SHANKS WAS STILL HARD AT WORK when an old Ford Econoline arrived at the ranch and was let through the front gate by security guards doubling as laborers upgrading a stone fence that surrounded the property. Rudy was driving the van, with Jimbo riding shotgun. Otto Bendellan, Claudette and Fabyan were in the back seat, watching over Maria and Veronica, who both lay on the floor. The prisoners were still bound hand and foot, but the gags had been removed.

"You'll never get away with this," Maria told her captors. "My brother will see to that."

"He will?" Claudette said, a sparkle of amusement in her eyes. "Tell me, sweetheart, have you given any thought to *why* he's not here with you and your friend?"

"What do you mean?" Fear washed across the young woman's face.

"They killed him," Veronica guessed, tears creeping down her cheeks. "Just like they're going to kill us."

"No! It's not true!" Maria looked at Fabyan. "Please, mister. We don't know anything about what you're up to. Just let us go. We won't talk."

"Then shut up!" Fabyan snapped. Although everyone else had managed some semblance of sleep on the flight out here, he'd been up all night, trying to reassess his position within the syndicate in the wake of recent events. His personal *soldati* had been decimated to the point that he could count his henchmen on his fingers. Since Felsur had begun spilling to the grand jury, the likelihood of the imprisoned mob underbosses staying behind bars was almost a moot point. It was bad enough he'd failed them thus far. If there was an expected scrambling for advancement within the organization in the aftermath of Felsur's confessions, Fabyan could expect little support in holding his position. At best, he figured to be phased out of the families' main operations and put in charge of some rinky-dink turf that would lead to nowhere. At worst . . . well, life was cheap in his line of work, especially to those who no longer commanded respect, and none of the ways mob misfits died were very pretty.

Of course, with the anthrax bombs successfully seized, Fabyan had a potent trump card in his hands, and if he played that card right, all the setbacks of previous days would be forgotten. He could come out of this in fine shape. It wasn't inconceivable that a day might come that he'd have the same title as the imprisoned overlords he was supposed to spring. *Sottocapo.* Underboss.

Rudy stopped the van near the side entrance to the ranch house. He and Jimbo got out and dragged the two prisoners from the vehicle.

"Bastards!" Veronica shouted. Both girls struggled but were easily subdued. Otto and Fabyan reapplied gags over the women's mouths while they were held in place.

"You're only making it rougher on yourselves," Claudette advised the prisoners.

Maria tried to scream through her gag. Fabyan reached over and cuffed her sharply with the back of his hand. As the girl stumbled back into Jimbo's arms from the force of the blow, Fabyan pulled out a Glock 17 service pistol and placed the barrel against her right temple.

"I told you to shut up!" he raged.

Stunned into silence, neither prisoner resisted as they were unceremoniously slung over the shoulders of their captors and hauled into the house. Sam was already back, having accompanied the chopper with the anthrax bombs. He dragged on a cigarette in the living room as he saw the women brought in.

"Ah, our little film stars," he chortled.

"I take it you got back all right," Claudette told Sam. "Where's Shanks?"

"Playing mad scientist out in the barn," Sam reported.

"Tell him I want to see him," Fabyan said.

Sam got up from his chair and put on his down vest. He paused to finger Maria's chin as soon as Rudy had set her down. "Pretty face."

Maria looked away from the cameraman, who laughed lightly on his way out of the house.

"Yeowwww!" Jimbo howled as Veronica kneed him in the groin the moment he unslung her from his shoulder. Furious, he shoved her across the living room into a well-worn sofa. Rudy guided Maria into a nearby chair.

"Well, you really don't give us much choice," Claudette said, going through her purse for a syringe and a fluid-filled vial. Rudy and Jimbo held the girls down as Claudette gave them both injections. It took less than thirty seconds for the drug to take effect, sapping the prisoners' strength without rendering them unconscious. "This batch is heroin, girls. Have fun...."

Leaving the captives, Claudette led Fabyan and Otto into the adjacent den, where they fixed themselves drinks and began to discuss their next move. They were interrupted moments later by the arrival of Kenneth Shanks. He was a short man, incredibly homely, his sparse hair dyed a bizarre shade of henna. His white lab coat was an inadequate buffer against the wintry chill outside, and he shivered as he walked to the bar and poured himself a glass of sherry.

"Well?" Fabyan asked him. "What's with the bombs?"

Shanks beamed happily, exposing a set of crooked, yellow teeth. "They'll suit our purposes nicely. I can have everything ready in two days, three at the most."

"Well, that's the best goddamn news I've heard all week." Fabyan raised his glass. "Cheers!"

The others joined him in the toast. After he downed his sherry, Shanks glanced into the living room and saw the two bound girls. He smiled again, then turned to Claudette. "You *did* say I'd be provided with a few diversions while I was out here, didn't you?"

Claudette smiled back at him. "Take your pick."

Shanks looked the girls over again. He wasn't cold anymore. A hot flush rippled through him, and he could feel his pulse quickening. "Decisions, decisions...perhaps I'll have them both."

17

Although she had been unconscious throughout her brush with death, something in Lao Ti's inner being must have had a glimpse of the afterlife and decided it wasn't time to make that journey, because in the ten hours after she suffered cardiac arrest, her condition improved immensely. She was still on the critical list, but her doctors had ceased speaking in terms of certain doom. The word "miracle" came up several times. She was even well enough to meet with her male counterparts before they headed out to Indiana. They found her weak but in good spirits, able to force a smile behind her oxygen mask when they walked in the room.

"I obviously haven't died and gone to heaven."

Caught off guard, the men broke out laughing.

"Hope you aren't disappointed," Brognola said.

She moved her head slightly from side to side. "I'll probably be reincarnated as a mushroom, so I'm in no hurry to leave just yet."

Schwarz glanced over at Lyons. "Maybe they gave her blood from a comedian."

Lao Ti's hand was resting next to the adjustment switch for her bed, and she pushed a button to help her sit up. "They think I'll get feeling back in my legs in a few days," she told the others.

"No need to rush things," Brognola responded. "You earned a vacation."

"Maybe so," she sighed, "but I let you guys down."

"No way, sister," Grimaldi said.

"He's right," Lyons insisted. "If you hadn't warned us and clipped that one guy on the hill, me and Schwarz would be worm bait right about now. We owe you one."

"Besides," Gadgets said, "we just found out the Politician's been playing hooky, so we're going to go drag his ass back on the roster. We'll be able to squeak by."

"Hooky?"

"Long story." Schwarz filled her in with the basics about Blancanales's ill-fated film job and the seizure of the anthrax bombs in Terre Haute. When he had finished, Lao Ti shook her head.

"How terrible," she said. "I hope you didn't let him stay in jail overnight just so you could see me."

Lyons shook his head. "They kept him overnight for observation at the hospital in Terre Haute. Besides, we had a few loose ends to tie up here."

"Whatever happened with Felsur?" Lao Ti wanted to know.

"He gave his testimony, then changed his mind about going free," Brognola said. He briefly explained about the threat sent on Nan Felsur's head, then concluded, "They've got him and his wife stashed away in the basement of the Justice Department back in Washington until this whole thing runs its course."

Lao Ti looked past the men. The window shades were open and she could see the sun trying to shine through a clot of thick, dark clouds. "What a world we live in," she said to no one in particular.

A doctor came into the room, carrying a clipboard. Behind him, an orderly wheeled in a tray filled with medical instruments.

"I'm going to have to ask you gentlemen to leave," the doctor told Lao Ti's visitors. The men exchanged farewells with her and filed out of the room. Lyons was the last to leave.

"Hang tough," he told her.

"Stay hard," she replied, smiling again through her clear green mask.

"OKAY, HOTSHOT," Lieutenant Lanski drawled as he un-locked the handcuffs chaining Blancanales to the hospital bed. "You got a clean bill of health except for your leg, and they say you were getting around on that before the swim, so we're going downtown."

A nurse pushed a wheelchair up to the bed as Pol swung his legs around and cast a sour eye at Lanski and Jensen.

"Any chance I can dress first?" he asked, tugging at his hospital gown. "I mean, you wouldn't want me to die of pneumonia before you get to show me off to your boss, would you?"

Lanski shrugged. "Be doing the taxpayers a favor."

Jensen opened a closet and tossed Blancanales his clothes, which had dried out but were wrinkled and soiled. "Don't worry, we've got nice clean outfits at the station."

The nurse stepped outside so Blancanales could change. His right leg felt as if someone was using it for a pin-cushion, but he wasn't about to give the officers the satis-faction of seeing his pain. Instead, he steeled himself with some of Carl Lyons's patented wisdom.

Nut up and do it.

"I take it Brognola hasn't gotten through to your people yet," Pol told the cops.

"Funny thing about that," Lanski mused. "We put a few calls through to Washington and weren't able to track down any Brognola."

"One guy thought it was something you put on a pizza," Jensen whispered.

"But then, I guess that was to be expected, right?" Lanski said. "You being part of a 'top-secret' agency and all. Better we should have called London and tried to get James Bond for a character reference, hmmm?"

"Or Maxwell Smart," Jensen ventured.

"Yeah," Lanski laughed, bending over for a better look at the shoes Blancanales was putting on. "Say, you wouldn't happen to have a phone tucked away there, would you? You could call the office again, try to butter up the boss."

Jensen pinched his fingers on either side of his nose to raise his voice in a mediocre imitation of Don Adams. "Sorry about that, chief!"

Blancanales smiled, but not at Jensen. He was looking past the cops at the man who'd just walked into the room. "Hey, chief!"

Hal Brognola was followed by a man in a tailored suit who Lanski and Jensen obviously recognized.

"What's up, Cap'n?" Lanski asked, already dreading the answer.

The man in the suit indicated Blancanales. "He's clear."

"Come on . . . you're kidding, right?"

The captain shook his head. The man next to him introduced himself to Lanski and Jensen. "Hi, I'm Hal Brognola. As you can see, I'm a little big to fit on a pizza."

"Oh, shit," Lanski moaned. "How long were you out there?"

"Long enough," Brognola assured him. He turned to Blancanales. "I convinced the captain here that the only things you might be guilty of are stupidity and gullibility. Fortunately, there's no law against either."

"No comment," Blancanales said. He quickly finished dressing and started for the door, telling Lanski and Jensen, "Thanks for the laughs, amigos. Next time I've got the blues I'll give you a call . . . on my shoe."

Once they were alone in the hallway, Brognola grumbled, "Well, Hollywood, any chance we can borrow you between features?"

"No need to rub it in," Pol told him, pressing for an elevator at the end of the corridor. "I learned my lesson, trust me."

On the way down to the ground floor, Brognola unwrapped a cigar and rolled it between his fingers. He briefed Pol on Lao Ti's progress, which was more promising than anything they'd come up with in their search for Maria, Veronica and the missing anthrax.

"We found out the weapons came from a supply officer skimming down at the Crane Naval Depot," the chief elaborated. "They found his body along with that of some guy named Nick Scurry."

"Scurry the gofer," Blancanales said.

"You know him?"

"Yeah, he was part of the film crew."

The elevator doors opened, letting the men out into the lobby. "I already took care of your paperwork, so we can just leave," Brognola said, leading the way to the nearest exit. "As for your film crew, we checked out some of the stuff left behind at the lot you mentioned and traced a few things to a camera shop owned by one of our favorite people."

"That Fabyan guy you told me about on the phone?"

Brognola nodded, holding the door open for Blancanales. "Yeah, he's the common denominator in all this shit. They tell me he's a short guy with a Napoleon complex."

"I think I saw him on the set," Blancanales said, recalling the limo that had showed up the same day he'd gone over the weapon supply list Otto and Mae had given him.

Mae.

He felt ashamed at how readily he'd let her dupe him, especially when he thought of all the sexual chemistry that had been cooked up between them. God, what a fool he'd been, motivated by his glands, thinking with that brain between his legs.

Lyons, Grimaldi and Schwarz were waiting in a rental car in front of the hospital. As Brognola and Blancanales got in, Pol noticed a definite lack of enthusiasm at his return.

"Yeah, yeah," he said with mock excitement, "I'm glad to be back too, guys, really."

Lyons gave Blancanales a look that quickly wiped the smirk off his face. "Pol, your sister's friend just turned up in a trash can with a blackmail note."

"*Madre de Dios*..." Pol could barely speak. "Where?"

"In the trunk of a stolen car they found ditched somewhere in Death Valley."

"What'd the note say?" Brognola asked.

"They want Felsur and the family dons," Schwarz said, "or else they're going to detonate the anthrax bombs aboveground over a storm front so they'll get spread around when it rains. Washington figures they could end up killing millions...."

18

Actually, it had been more than a mere garbage can Veronica Rammite's violated body had been stuffed in. The container was a seamless barrel normally used for the storage of toxic waste. Since organized crime had long been involved in cheap, illegal means of disposing of such wastes, there had been few problems in securing one of the barrels for use in delivering Fabyan's blackmail demands. Of course, the main reason for using such a secure container was that Veronica's unclothed body had been laid to rest with an exposed sample of anthrax that Kenneth Shanks had extracted from one of the stolen missiles. Sam had taken Polaroid shots of the entire proceedings, in which all the participants except Veronica were well disguised in full-length anti-CBW suits that included hooded face masks.

Driving the Ford van from Claudette Simms's Wyoming ranch with the entombed body carefully secured in back, Bendellan and Jimbo had traveled as far as Las Vegas before stealing a '72 Olds parked outside a topless bar on the north strip. With the barrel transferred to the trunk of the Olds, the two men had driven separately across the border into California, abandoning the sedan under cover of night near the base of Death Valley's appropriately named Funeral Mountains.

On their way out of Death Valley, the two men had stopped at a mailbox in Furnace Creek to send off envelopes to the Los Angeles affiliates of each of the three major television networks. Because Fabyan was certain the authorities would try to suppress any news of the blackmail scheme for fear that public hysteria would hamper the government's negotiating leverage, each envelope contained some of Sam's photos, a list of Fabyan's blackmail demands and details about where Veronica's body had been abandoned.

As a further means of blowing the lid off the story and assuring that the media take notice, Bendellan and Jimbo had stopped off at a truck stop in Barstow long enough for Otto to place an anonymous phone call to a tabloid reporter in Vegas with a reputation for foolhardiness in the pursuit of a scoop.

When they reached Los Angeles shortly after dawn and switched on the news at the Travelodge they'd checked into, the two men learned their ploy had succeeded beyond their wildest expectations. During an uninterrupted fifteen-minute segment, it was divulged that the National Informer's Las Vegas-based reporter, Everett Thompson, had taken a staff cameraman with him to Death Valley following an early-morning phone tip that they would find the body of a slain showgirl. Arriving at the scene without having informed the police and finding the Old's trunk unlocked, they had taken it upon themselves to break the barrel's seal. After filming the body and the blackmail note, the reporter had sent the cameraman off to meet with their editor in Las Vegas while he stayed behind to protect the exclusivity of his story, unaware that they had both been exposed to the anthrax virus. By the time he'd returned to Las Vegas, the cameraman was suffering from contamination symptoms, which included convulsions and bloody discharge. His editor had admitted him to a local hospital and notified the police, but not before he'd broken the story to the Informer's national desk and arrangements had been made to sell photo rights to the networks. Everett Thompson had been dead next to the Olds when police in special anti-CBW gear had arrived at the drop site. That entire section of Death Valley was now under quarantine, and the authorities knew they had a monumental crisis on their hands.

"Not a bad night's work, eh, Otto?" Jimbo told his partner as he stretched out on his bed and yawned. "Shit, I'm beat."

"Go ahead and crash," Bendellan told him, splashing some cold water on his face and then toweling off before raiding his coat pocket for a couple tabs of Benzedrine. "I still want to take care of a few things."

THE INDUSTRIAL AREA of Canoga Park was located a few miles north of Jorges and Anna Blancanales' home, along a corridor that ran between Topanga Canyon Boulevard and Canoga Avenue. Unlike the landscaped and more architecturally imposing complexes down the road in Woodland Hills, business sites in Canoga Park were first and foremost utilitarian. Whole city blocks were given over to fenced-in clusters of drab cinder-block buildings that provided work and storage space to enterprises as varied as computer design, auto body repair, contact lens crafting and the assembly-line creation of dolls based on Saturday-morning cartoon characters. There were few retail outlets in the area and no tourist attractions to speak of, so traffic tended to be sparse between the early-morning and late-afternoon rush hours.

For the Los Angeles Cinzo family, blood relatives to the Cleveland Cinzos that Dave X. Fabyan worked for, this low-key, out-of-the-way industrial sector was an ideal base for many of their West Coast operations. If you were a made man with the right family connections, there were any number of legitimate shops you could drop in at and be led through inner doors to someone who could help you out with a service that wasn't mentioned on the outdoor sign.

You could buy a gun at a toy warehouse, fence hot stereos at a place that made accessories for patio furniture or place bets with a bookie who fronted as an appliance repairman.

Bendellan pulled through a gateway and parked the Ford Econoline outside a paint-and-body shop. He walked past a pair of middle-aged, stoop-backed illegal Mexicans sanding down a refurbished Mustang and headed into the garage area, where a long-haired man with tattooed forearms was welding the mangled front fender of a white Mercedes. He motioned for Otto to wait a moment as he finished his work, then turned down the flame on his acetylene torch and flipped up his protective visor.

"Otto, my man! What it is!"

"Hello, Bart," Bendellan responded with considerably less enthusiasm.

"Lookin' for the boss?"

"Of course."

"He's in the usual place." Bart tapped the fresh seam he'd just burnt into the Mercedes. "He did this on the way to work today. Clipped some kid on a skateboard and damn near sheared a hydrant. Man, I wish I could have seen that!"

"I'll talk to you later, Bart, okay?"

Bart looked at the briefcase Otto was carrying and grinned knowingly. "Got some new stuff, huh?"

"You're here to fix cars, right?" There was more than just irritation in Bendellan's voice.

Bart knew he'd overstepped his bounds, so he merely nodded and turned back to his work. Otto walked away from the mechanic and sidestepped a clutter of tools and equipment before reaching a metal door that led to a back hallway and a flight of steps. He went up to the second floor and knocked on another thick door. There was a peephole mounted in the door, and Otto stood back on the landing so that he could be seen easily.

Twenty seconds later, the door opened and a short, stubby man with unwashed hair and a two-day growth of beard waved Bendellan inside. Wes Conzi liked to think he had the Don Johnson look down pat, but he looked more like a transient determined not to let winning the state lottery affect his life-style.

"Hey, Bender, good to see ya."

"Same here," Bendellan said as they pumped hands.

The entire second story of the building was devoted to the Conzi family's primary source of income on the West Coast—pornographic movie distribution. There was machinery on hand for duplicating films in various formats, most commonly videocassettes. Artwork, labeling, packaging—all of it was done here, creating a constant flow of product for the pruriently inclined to view at their local triple-*X* theater or in the comfort of their own home. A crew of seventeen employees was at work at various stations, and few of them bothered glancing up at the man who'd just walked in. They knew from experience that ignorance was a good thing in this business.

"C'mon, let's go to my office and see watcha got."

Bendellan followed Conzi to a corner room that was partitioned off from the main work area. Once they were inside, the pornographer closed the door behind him and dropped his happy facade.

"Fuck, Bender, what the hell's going on with Fabyan? I heard the news about that poison shit on the way to work. I damn near totaled my car."

"So I heard."

"Man, they aren't really gonna put that shit in the clouds, are they? They say that rain would drop people like flies wherever it landed!" Conzi was definitely rattled. "I mean, I like my cousin and all, but hell, he ain't worth *that* much."

Bendellan set his briefcase on Conzi's desk and opened it, taking out one of the four videocassettes he'd brought with him. "I really don't think it'll ever reach that point, but if it does, we'll probably spike clouds that aren't heading for any big cities. Kill a few cows in Kansas and they'll get the idea." He slipped the tape into a VCR resting on top of a color TV with a thirty-inch screen. As he flipped the controls, he reminded Conzi, "But that's not why I'm here, right?"

"Yeah," the pornographer conceded, bringing himself under control. "Business as usual."

There were two plush leather chairs facing the television. The men sat down and both lit up cigarettes as they watched Kenneth Shanks drool over Veronica and Maria. The girls were just barely conscious; both were in various stages of undress, still bound and gagged.

"Guy's a little old for this, don't you think?" Conzi said.

Bendellan took a slow drag on his cigarette and tapped ash into a large ceramic tray on the coffee table in front of them. Like Conzi, he was looking at the film not as a patron of the arts but as a businessman.

"I just read where they say thirty percent of porn rentals are by men over sixty," Bendellan said. "Might cheer 'em up to see one of their own involved."

"Maybe you got a point there," Conzi said, eyes still on the screen. He broke out laughing. "*He* sure does."

Shanks had obviously been unaware that his debauchery was being filmed. He sang in short, nonsensical rhymes as he violated his victims.

"That chick on the right is hot," Conzi said, indicating Maria Blancanales. "Good equipment. Nice eyes."

"This is the tamest of the batch," Bendellan remarked. "Trim it a little and it'll work for over-the-counter sales."

"*Grampa's Little Girls*," Conzi murmured, trying out possible titles. "Or maybe *Dirty Old Gland*."

Bendellan shook his head. "Bad marketing. You gotta play it up to the guys buying it, remember? Something more like *He Taught Them Well*."

"Bullshit, that sounds like some sequel to *Goodbye, Mr. Chips*."

"*Good Lay, Mr. Chips*?"

"Yeah, that's better." Conzi grabbed a remote control and switched off the tape. When he looked over at Bendellan, there was a hint of anticipation in his eyes. "You said that's the tamest one you brought. Got some of the good stuff?"

They both knew what he was talking about.

"Two," Bendellan said, reaching for his briefcase.

"Oh, no," Conzi groaned. "You didn't off that spic babe right off, did you?"

"No," Bendellan assured him. "Claudette figures she's got a lot of use left before we're done with her...."

19

Nash Felsur didn't taste the Chinese food that had been brought to him and his wife at their new quarters in the basement of the Justice building in Washington, D.C. The egg rolls and spicy beef might as well have been texturized cardboard. His senses had been dulled earlier by chemotherapy sessions and radiation treatments, but it was the grisly death of his daughter that had finished them off. He'd gotten through his appearance before the grand jury because rage and a desire for vengeance had spurred him on, but now he could barely summon even the strength for hatred.

Why Nan?

He should have died. He deserved to. Looking back over his years with the syndicate, he lost track of the number of times he'd cheated death. The shoot-out at Battino's restaurant, when a bullet meant for his heart had been deflected by his cigarette case. That night in Indianapolis when on a whim he'd sent Joey Piano-Teeth to fetch his car, unaware that Bad Tad Calder had rigged a bomb to the ignition. The crash landing of Bison-breath Avery's chopper when a tinkered fuel hose broke. Hell, that was just the tip of the iceberg, and those were only the instances when he knew he'd been targeted for elimination. There were probably at least as many botched attempts he had never found out about.

Yeah, he'd had a charmed life, and what did he have to show for it? His pride and joy with her head chopped off and used for notepaper. His wife half-dead with grief, trying her best to keep from blaming him for what had happened. And forced to live in this damn underground bunker like a sewer rat.

During one idle moment after he'd turned himself in, Felsur had calculated that more than twenty million dollars in cash had passed through his fingers during his rise through the ranks of the family. Blood money, earned off the pain of others. What he wouldn't give to have those years back, to live them out in some unknown town as just another poor wage earner, struggling to get by and loving every minute of it because at the end of each day he'd come home to a family and a house he could call his own. The good, simple things—he'd never really appreciated them until they'd been taken away.

He looked over at his wife, who stared vacantly at the floor, nibbling on a teriyaki chicken wing. "You shoulda left me that first time we fought over my business," he told her, breaking the silence that engulfed them.

"I would have," she responded. "But I loved you. I still do, Nash."

"Why?" he shouted, tossing his plate aside and getting up from the cramped table in the corner of the dark cubicle that passed as their living room. "I done nothing but bring you pain."

She moved over and put her hands on his shoulders, soothing him. "It's like the preacher said, honey. 'For better or for worse.' We'll get through this. Somehow."

Nash shook his head in disbelief. "You gotta be crazy...."

BLANCANALES WAS GRAPPLING with a guilt of his own. Having allowed himself to be duped into plotting the anthrax seizure, he'd also played an unwitting part in helping the perpetrators escape. Thinking they had their best suspect in custody, Pol reasoned, the authorities had probably relaxed their search for the others long enough to let them get across the state line and to another part of the country entirely. True, Veronica's body had turned up in central California, but he knew those responsible for her death could be anywhere, plotting ways to unleash the deadly rains in case their bluff was called and the syndicate chieftains remained in police custody.

He had to do something.

Brognola had brought Able Team back to Stony Man Farm following disclosure of Veronica Rammite's death and the issuance of the syndicate's ultimatum. While Lyons and Schwarz remained at the compound to await further word, Grimaldi flew Brognola and Blancanales to Washington. Stony Man's chief of operations had been assigned by the President to chair the ad hoc group in charge of the anthrax crisis. Grimaldi sat in as an aviation specialist to help anticipate possible scenarios that the mob might attempt to carry out its threats.

As for Blancanales, he reported to the Justice Department, where he spent the better part of three hours helping identification experts put together composite sketches of everyone involved in the *You Ran, Iran* scam he'd been the fall guy for.

When the composites were completed, Blancanales was escorted to the basement of the building and taken to the Felsurs' makeshift quarters. After being introduced to the mobster and his wife, Pol sat down with them and explained the reason for his visit.

When Blancanales was finished, Nash said, "If there's anything I can do to save your sister from what happened to my daughter, count me in." The dying man clutched his wife's hand, trying to rally their strength with a resolve to do what was right.

"These are the people we're looking for," Pol said, handing the composites to Felsur. "Do you know any of them?"

Felsur held the simulated mug shots at arm's length, going through them one by one, shaking his head at each face. "My guess is they're *soldati*," he theorized. "They don't work directly for Fabyan or I'd at least recognize— Oh, no. No..."

The bluish veins in Felsur's neck stood out, and he began to tremble with an incredible fury. From his lips spewed a torrent of profanities in what Blancanales guessed must be Sicilian dialect. The man's wife pleaded with him to calm down, and he eventually complied, although anger was still present in his voice as he stabbed an accusatory finger at the only composite of a woman.

"Claudette Simms," he hissed. "Of course it would be her!"

"What about her?"

Felsur turned to his wife and said something in his native tongue. She shook her head, and there was a brief argument before she finally got up and walked to the other side of the chamber, arms folded across her chest. Felsur leaned close to Blancanales and lowered his voice.

"She is poison, this woman," he said, pointing again at the likeness of Claudette. "She does some work for the family, but she is not one of us. We wouldn't have her. Her specialty is smut films."

"Pornography?" Blancanales thought of his sister at the mercy of Claudette and cringed.

"I'm not talking about the kind of dirty pictures you see at bachelor parties," Felsur said. He glanced over his shoulder to make sure his wife wasn't within earshot before continuing. His voice cracked slightly from the effort needed to rage in a whisper. "She has women killed on camera after they've been molested and tortured. The bitch! My daughter, my lovely Nancy, can you imagine what they did to her?"

Pol swallowed hard. His imagination was conjuring up unspeakable tableaux, flashing images of young girls' faces in the throes of unbearable agonies. He saw Nan Felsur. And he saw his sister. And Claudette, the woman he had almost slept with, standing off on the sidelines, recording the tortures she had instigated.

"Where can I find her?" he asked Felsur.

The old man could only shrug. "She's West Coast, out of my territory. But I've heard that many of her films have mountains in them. The Rockies, I think...."

Pol put the composites away and stood up, thanking Felsur for his help and apologizing for putting him through such an ordeal.

"Do me a favor when you find her," Felsur implored. "See that she dies."

Pol Blancanales had never in his life thought he would undertake a hit on behalf of a member of organized crime, but before he left the cubicle he nodded at Nash Felsur and told him, "She'll pay...."

20

Maria Blancanales felt sick. She was in pain and she was confused. How many days had passed since she'd first been abducted? Was it daytime now? When had she been dreaming and when had the terrible things happening to her been real? Where was Veronica? Where was Rosie?

She was lying on a bed of straw in the same stable where Nan Felsur had been raped and butchered. She could hear voices and see shapes all around her, but nothing registered clearly. Her hearing, her vision, her sense of touch—everything seemed distorted. She tried to call out for help, but her mouth wouldn't cooperate. She could make only strained, guttural sounds that gave way to sobs of despair.

"I think we ought to let up on her for a while," Sam said, standing back from the camera and looking at Maria, who twisted helplessly in the stall where they had shoved her after dragging her into the stable. Her body was bruised, and dark circles hung below her sunken, teary eyes. "She's too strung out to be good for anything right now."

"Maybe so," Claudette concurred. She tossed a woollen blanket to Rudy, who was working the lights. "Take her back to the house and get some food into her, then put her out for the night. A couple of days' rest and we'll start in again."

Rudy went over and folded Maria into the blanket and carried her out the barn's side door. Sam began striking the set while Claudette lit a cigarette and went in the opposite direction, heading down the main hallway.

Dave X. Fabyan was sitting in a small alcove halfway down the corridor, scribbling notes on a pad as he watched the all-weather channel on a small color television hooked up to the ranch's satellite dish.

"Target practice?" she asked, dropping into one of the chairs next to the *caporegime*.

Fabyan nodded. "Lotta rain in the forecast. Plenty of places to choose from if they force our hand." He pointed to a map of the United States when it flashed on the screen. "Pacific Northwest looks promising. So does that front moving over Oklahoma."

Claudette noticed the time. "They still have a few hours to give in," she said. "You think they will?"

"Depends," Fabyan said. "If they think it through, they gotta know that keeping a few *sottocapi* on ice isn't going to put us out of business, so letting 'em go seems like a small price to pay, considering the alternatives."

"But let's be realistic," Claudette said. "They're already pegging this a terrorist act, and their policy has always been not to cut deals."

The stocky *capo* snorted derisively. "C'mon, Claudette, we both know better than that. They talk tough, but when push comes to shove they got their tail between their legs. What do you think all that Iran arms-sale shit was about?"

Claudette had been waiting for this moment ever since Fabyan had first approached her for help with the anthrax heist. For her, possession of so powerful a weapon was wasted as a bargaining chip for the release of old-guard bosses. She thought there were far more profitable possibilities.

"Tell me, Dave," she said, putting a soft edge on her voice to make sure she had his attention. "What would happen inside the organization if Conzi and the others stayed behind bars?''

Fabyan looked hard at the woman. "I know what you're getting at, and don't think I haven't thought about it myself. But just because they're in prison doesn't mean they don't still call the shots. One hint that I'm trying to jump ranks behind their backs and some morning three guys will show up in my bedroom ready for the Italian rope trick. You know that one?''

Claudette nodded quietly. Of course she knew it. The victim is greeted by three acquaintances. He shakes somebody's hand, hi, how ya doin', and the next thing he knows two of the guys are holding him down while the third slips a noose around his neck from behind and starts pulling. They always die with a look of surprise, losing control of their bowels and bladder. She'd used the technique to good effect on women in some of her snuff films.

"But what if you did all you could and the government still wouldn't budge?" Claudette said. "What then?"

"Like I said, they'd still run the show from their cells," Fabyan said. "It'd be just an inconvenience."

"Fifteen years to life of inconvenience?" Claudette asked. "Do you really think that the whole organization's going to stay put?"

"All right," Fabyan snapped. "There's gonna be a lot of jockeying for power, okay? I ain't a complete idiot. I'll look out for number one, don't worry."

"I wasn't worried," Claudette assured him. "Just curious. How would you go about it?"

"That's my problem, isn't it?" Fabyan glared at Claudette. "What the fuck are you driving at, anyway?"

Claudette remained calm. She took one last long draw on her cigarette and crushed it out on the floor.

"You know, Dave, there's markets for these anthrax bombs," she finally said. "Iraq, the Sikhs, Moslem fanatics—they'd all pay top dollar for a chance to kill each other as quickly as possible."

"That so?" Fabyan was skeptical. "And I suppose you got a little black book with all their names in it."

"Something like that." Claudette smiled enigmatically. "You'd be surprised at the wide range of contacts you make in my line of business. Cosa Nostra is not my only client, you know."

"And you think by putting me in touch with some of these special friends of yours I can move this anthrax for enough cash to buy me more influence here at home?"

"It's something to think about," Claudette told him.

"Yeah," Fabyan said. "Maybe it is at that."

Before they were able to lay any further ground work for this new option, Rudy returned to the barn and tracked them down, his face flushed with excitement. "They're giving in!" he exclaimed, waving a newspaper in front of Claudette and Fabyan.

"What?" Fabyan said.

"Check it out!"

Rudy handed the paper to Fabyan. It was the final edition of the *Denver Post*, one of seventeen newspapers throughout the country that Fabyan had designated as the forum through which the government was to respond to his demands for the release of his superiors. As prescribed in the demands, the response was listed in the classifieds under Lost and Found. It was a coded message, translatable only by the parties involved. To anyone without the code, the ad was for a lost diamond brooch with a lot of sentimental value to the owner. The information between the lines told Fabyan another story.

"I don't believe it!" he muttered. "They're willing to negotiate."

"You're kidding," Claudette said.

Fabyan shook his head, pointing to the ad. "The only thing they won't agree to is releasing Felsur. And they want the anthrax back, too."

"Well," Claudette said. "This certainly changes things...."

Fabyan looked over the ad again, trying to read between the lines. "It doesn't smell right. I think they're just trying to buy time."

"And put some pressure on you," Claudette said after a few moments of speculation.

"How so?"

"If Cinzo and the others know the Feds are willing to deal, it just serves notice to you and all the other *capo-regimes*. No power moves. You've got to play along."

"Shit," Fabyan grumbled. He flashed a sour smile at Claudette. "Just when I thought you and I were on to something."

"We can still make that work," Claudette said.

"Not if we have to give all the anthrax back."

Claudette reminded him, "We still have Shanks. Keep him happy and he'll help us come up with another supply. It'll take more time, that's all."

Fabyan mulled over the paper again. "And not getting Felsur's no real problem. We can just wait till they put him back on the streets and then we'll sniff him out."

"What about witness relocation?" Rudy put in. "Won't they give him plastic surgery and a new name?"

"That won't help him if we want him bad enough."

Claudette lit up another cigarette and snapped off the television. "Then I guess we better put our heads together and plan the exchange. Rudy, go put a call through to Los Angeles and try to reach Otto."

"Will do."

As Rudy disappeared down the hallway, Claudette stayed behind with Fabyan. "Look at it this way, Dave," she said encouragingly. "If they do get released, your stock's going to shoot way up with them."

Fabyan nodded. "Yeah, it sure as hell will. Goddamn, I just can't lose, can I?"

21

Backtracking to square one, Blancanales returned to Los Angeles to begin his search for Claudette Simms and his missing sister. His tender leg still hurt like hell, but he would live with it. Nothing was going to hold him back from seeing this one through. Gadgets Schwarz and Carl Lyons were with him, more than glad for a chance to lend him their help. Of course, with Maria's disappearance directly linked with the anthrax dilemma, Able Team was involved in more than a mere personal case. If anything, this was one of the more crucial of their ongoing attempts to tip the scales of justice a bit more in favor of good.

This phase of their mission got off to an unpromising start, however.

Not surprisingly, when the three men went to the building on Sunset Boulevard where Blancanales had been interviewed for the film job, they found new tenants in the midst of redecorating the offices that had previously been used by YouRan Productions.

Referred to the building manager, an officious-looking woman in her late fifties, they found few leads to go on. As the manager explained it, Claudette, using her Mae Jung pseudonym, had sublet the offices from another outfit after answering an advertisement in the trades. It had been a cash arrangement, and the little paperwork that had been drawn up was worthless, since a few checkup calls confirmed that most of the information was bogus.

"Unfortunately, things like this happen more than you'd think in Hollywood," the manager explained apologetically. "Would-be producers lay out some quick cash on appearances and hope they'll swing some sweetheart deal. It usually doesn't work, and they slink away to lick their wounds before trying it again."

"There were a lot of furnishings in that office," Blancanales mentioned. "Any idea when that was slinked away?"

The woman nodded. "Four days ago."

"After hours?"

"Yes. We usually insist on that so our other clients don't have their business disrupted."

Blancanales was on a roll. "And I assume there was a security guard on duty at the time to keep an eye on things."

The woman nodded again. "Harvey Gibbs. He's on duty downstairs if you want to speak to him."

Pol thanked the woman for her help and the three men took the elevator down to the ground floor. Gibbs was at his post near the main doorway, chatting with two of the parking attendants. When asked about the evacuation of YouRan Productions's office, the guard wasn't much help. He couldn't recall the name of the moving company, and the head of the outfit had filled the sign-in ledger with indecipherable handwriting. Fortunately, Blancanales had brought along copies of the composites he'd had drawn up in Washington, and Gibbs fingered Jimbo, Rudy and Otto Bendellan as three of the men who had been in on the move.

"Hell, we already figured that," Schwarz sulked after Able Team thanked Gibbs for his help and headed outside.

"Hey, amigo," one of the parking attendants whispered, following the men out of the building. Blancanales turned and recognized the same young man who'd parked his father's car the day of his fateful interview with Claudette Simms.

"Yeah?" Pol said, motioning for Lyons and Schwarz to wait.

"I heard you talking to him," the carhop said, jerking his head to indicate Gibbs. "Maybe I got some information for you."

"What kind of information?"

The attendant grinned. He lured Able Team into a niche between the building and the parking garage, away from pedestrian traffic. "You got a picture of President Grant, maybe?" he bartered.

"Huh?" Blancanales didn't know what the hell the kid was talking about.

Lyons did. He said, "He wants fifty bucks to talk." The Ironman reached for his wallet and pulled out two twenties, telling the kid, "We'll give you one Andrew Jackson to open your mouth and another if anything interesting comes out of it."

The youth sighed. "I like President Grant better."

"Okay, sixty bucks," Schwarz said, coming up with another twenty. "Just make sure you're worth it."

The youth took Gadgets's twenty and kept his eyes on Lyons as he talked. "I was still here when they were moving. They had one guy hurt his back when they was half done, and they asked me to help finish. I tell them I like President Grant and they tell me I got a job.

"So I'm working with them and I got my ears open. The two biggest guys, they keep talking about broads. We're lugging this big desk and one guy says something like 'We oughta film some broad laid out on this.'"

"Just get to the punch line, okay?" Lyons interrupted. "We aren't paying you by the word."

"Hey, I'm getting there, okay?" The attendant made a face at Lyons before continuing. "Anyway, I figure these guys must do fuck flicks, right? I ask 'em if the pay's good, and the big guy tells me, 'Yeah, lotta tips and all you can eat!' Real comedian, huh? Well, I tell 'em I'm a good stud. They tell me to mind my own business, but hey, I want in on this action. I seen those flicks, man. Yum yum!''

Blancanales took a sudden step forward and grabbed the attendant's lapels, almost lifting him off his feet in his rage. "What's your information, amigo?''

The attendant's eyes bulged. "Easy, man,'' he pleaded. "This ain't my coat.''

"This ain't your day, either, if you think you can bait us for money and walk away without a payoff,'' Blancanales advised him.

"Okay, okay.'' The youth waited until Blancanales let go of him, then brushed his coat and tried to regain his cool. "Look, I figured I wanted to check this thing out later, maybe get an in with somebody higher up. So when they aren't looking, I went looking through the desk. Got me a business card.'' He went through his wallet and pulled the card out. "It's up in the Valley, so I haven't been there yet.''

Blancanales looked at the business card and frowned. "This is for a body repair shop.''

"Yeah, I wondered about that, too. But flip it over.''

Pol checked the back of the card and saw a handwritten phone number, along with a name. "Wes Conzi,'' he read aloud, glancing at Schwarz and Lyons.

"It fits,'' Schwarz said.

"Thing is,'' the attendant added, "I tried calling up there to check things out and I dialed the number on front by mistake. I asked for Wes anyway, bluffing like I knew all about his business, you know, and he was there. Hung up on me right off, but he was there.''

"At the repair shop?''

The attendant bobbed his head. Without saying anything else, Lyons gave the kid the other forty bucks and Able Team headed for their car. The carhop realized they'd taken the business card with them, but he shrugged it off. "Probably woulda caught the clap, anyhow...."

ON THEIR WAY to the west end of the Valley, Able Team made a detour to Van Nuys, a city perhaps best known for late-night cruises of customized cars down its main thoroughfare. Lyons was driving their rental van and he parked near the police station on Van Nuys Boulevard. Gadgets and Blancanales went to a burger shop down the block while Lyons entered the station and asked at the main desk to see Bill Towers. He was sent down the hall to the detective's office, where Towers was telling one of his fellow officers that he was on his way out for lunch.

"How about if I buy?" Lyons said.

Towers spun around, startled by the sound of the other man's voice. A grin broke across his weary face. "Carl Lyons! Well, I'll be damned!"

"I'm sure you will," Lyons assured him as they shook hands. "I didn't think you could get any uglier than last time I saw you, Bill, but surprise, surprise."

"Yeah, fuck you, too," Towers laughed. "Just for that, you *will* pick up the tab."

Bill Towers and Carl Lyons went back a long way, starting with the years when they'd both been LAPD officers. For a long stint they'd been partners, and Towers said that tales of their escapades during that tumultuous period were still part of the local police folklore. Although they'd drifted out of touch when Lyons had shifted onto the course that eventually made him a member of Able Team, their paths had crossed several times in recent years. Twice they'd renewed their partnership in a temporary, unofficial capacity during brutal West Coast battles with underlings of Cuba's nefarious *Dirección General de Inteligencia*.

Things had been quiet for Towers of late, though, and his transfer to the Valley left him the feeling that he was turning soft. When he found out that Lyons was indirectly mixed up with the anthrax bomb scare that had LAPD and every law enforcement agency in the land working overtime, the detective had a ready response.

"I should have known."

On their way to the burger shop, Lyons filled him in with the details, particularly concerning Pol's sister and the porno ring headed up by Claudette Simms. When told about the suspected location of the ring's L.A. headquarters, Towers nodded his head.

"We've had that area under surveillance for months," he said. "Another couple weeks and we're going to raid that whole area with as many paddy wagons as we can muster."

Lyons looked at his friend. "We don't aim to wait that long. And after we're through, there probably won't be any need for paddy wagons."

"Why are you telling me this?" Towers wondered.

They joined Blancanales and Schwarz, who were sucking on chocolate shakes under a faded umbrella outside the burger joint.

"We want to handle this our way," Lyons told Towers. "I was hoping you could make sure the heat doesn't drop by and get in the way before we're finished."

Towers traded silent greetings with Lyons's cohorts as he considered his friend's request. "When's it going down?"

"No time like the present," Lyons said.

"How true." Towers smiled. "Well, I guess I'll be out to lunch longer than I expected."

"Meaning what?"

"Meaning if you want me to keep the other boys in blue away, I'm going to have to come along," Towers said.

"We want to handle this alone," Lyons reminded him.

"And I want to see if my heart still knows what it's like to tap dance on my rib cage," Towers replied evenly. "Look, you guys want dibs on the outset, fine. I'll cover your back and pick off any leftovers that come my way. Think it over while I order."

As Towers went up to the take-out window, Lyons looked at Blancanales and Schwarz. "Well?"

"Fine by me," Schwarz said.

Blancanales thought it over for a few seconds, then said, "If we're bringing along backup, no sense being half-assed about it. I know somebody else we could use...."

PETE BANFIELD DOUBLE-LOCKED the back door to his survivalist shop behind him. He walked with Pol to the van that was idling at the mouth of the alley. The vet's illegal PPSh-41 subgun was barely concealed under his jacket.

"Be nice to try this bastard out," he reflected. Before they joined the others inside the van, Pete added, "I appreciate your dealing me in, Pol. Especially since I was the one that got you started on this whole nightmare."

Once Banfield and Blancanales were in, Lyons headed off, turning onto Sherman Way and heading west. It was a little after two-thirty in the afternoon. Clouds from a Pacific storm front were rolling over the valley, which was one reason LAPD was so wary about the anthrax scare. One well-timed bomb blast above this cloud cover and a hard rain was gonna fall.

"Pete called the clerk who was on duty when the notice was posted," Pol told the others. "From the description he gave, it must have been Bendellan who dropped by."

"Makes sense," Schwarz said. "Hell, we're only a couple miles from the repair shop. It was a natural."

There was another address close to their target, and the closer they got to it, the more uneasy Blancanales felt. He didn't want to make that one extra stop, but the more he thought about it, the more he was sure he had to.

"Right at the next light," he told Lyons.

"But I thought we weren't turning until we got to Canoga."

"Just do it," Pol said. "It's personal."

"Your folks?"

"Yeah," Pol muttered.

"You sure you want to do that?" Schwarz asked him.

"I have to."

Pol directed Lyons to the address, and he pulled up into the driveway. Blancanales unslung the shoulder holster with his .45 before getting out of the car. "I won't be long."

Getting out of the van, Pol took a deep breath and started up the drive. He saw his mother through the front window and felt his face redden with shame. He'd already heard the pain in her voice when he had first called with the news, but the tortured look of agony on her face was something he could never have been prepared for. All in all, the few remaining steps to the front door turned into what felt like the longest walk Pol Blancanales had ever taken.

Jorges had joined Anna in the doorway. He opened the door for his son. There was pain in the old man's eyes, as well, but other, deeper emotions lurked in his gaze. Neither he nor Anna spoke at first. Pol didn't know what to say, either, but he forced out the first words that came into his head.

"I'm sorry." His voice was strained with emotion. "It's all my fault."

"Oh, Rosario..." Anna stepped forward and pulled her son into a tearful embrace. "Oh, my son..."

Jorges placed a hand on his son's shoulder. "You didn't know." For the first time in his life, Pol saw tears in his father's eyes. The old man's voice quavered slightly. "Don't blame yourself, son. We love you."

Pol wasn't sure which stunned him more, their failure to condemn him for what had happened or their emotional show of support. Speechless, he returned their embrace with his own. "I love you, too," he told them.

"There's still hope," Anna whispered. "I pray for the soul of her friend, but we must keep our faith that Maria will be all right."

"Yes, Mom."

When they finally withdrew from one another, Jorges glanced out the doorway and saw the van. He blinked away his tears and once more became the stoic patriarch. "Who are *they*?"

"Friends," Pol said. "We're on our way someplace, but I just wanted to stop by and see you first."

"Where are you going?" Anna asked worriedly.

"I'll be all right, Mom."

"You know where they are, don't you?" Jorges said. He stared defiantly at his son. "Answer me."

"I have to go," Pol said, backing away toward the door.

"Wait!" Jorges strode to the hall closet and jerked the door open. He reached in and pulled out a Winchester Model 70 Lightweight Carbine and several boxes of ammunition for the 6-shot magazine. "I'm going with you!"

"Pops, no..."

"I am your father, and Maria is my daughter!" Jorges thundered. "I'm going with you!"

One look in the old man's eyes and Pol knew that the decision had been made.

22

Bart the welder swilled the last of his beer and crushed the can in his monstrous fingers. Belching, he wound up and threw the aluminum wad across the garage, striking one of his fellow workers between the shoulder blades.

"Ouch!" the other man howled, whirling around. He was half a head shorter and fifty pounds lighter than Bart, but he was buffed out from the weight-lifting regimen at a local health spa and didn't look like the kind to be easily intimidated. "What's the big idea, greasehead?"

"You were snoring, Cobb," Bart complained. "Bad enough I gotta go half-deaf from all the noise you make when you're working. I don't need it when you're on break, too."

"If it gets too noisy, just poke your pecker in your ear," Cobb jibed. "It's small enough."

The two Mexican laborers snickered on the outdoor bench where they were finishing their lunch. Bart turned on them as he lit his acetylene torch. "You little shits think that's funny? You want funny, I'll torch you into refried beaners."

The two older men fell silent and headed over to finish work on Otto Bendellan's freshly repainted Ford Econoline, parked next to the Mustang in the shade of the two-story building. Safely out of the welder's earshot, they whispered to one another in Spanish, calling Bart choice names that might have lost something in the translation.

Wes Conzi's Mercedes was the only vehicle inside the three-car service area. As Bart and Cobb put aside their feuding and began working on the car, a late-model van rolled onto the lot at thirty miles an hour and swerved to a halt in the bay next to the Mercedes.

"What the fuck?" Bart exclaimed as he glanced up through his welding mask, lit torch in his hand.

Both the front and back passenger doors of the van swung open. Pol Blancanales and Gadgets Schwarz bolted out, each brandishing Kissingerized Colt .45s with fifteen-round magazines. Cobb was so taken by surprise that Pol was able to cuff him behind the head with the butt of his gun, dropping him to the concrete like deadweight.

Bart, with the Mercedes between him and the intruders, bought a few seconds by cranking up the gas on his torch and quickly waving it in front of him like a wand. The near-blinding light forced Pol and Gadgets to look away as Bart backed into the downstairs service office and clicked on a silent alarm.

His vision blurred by afterflashes from the torch, Gadgets nonetheless sprang forward, landing in a crouch on the hood of the Mercedes and leaving the auto in need of further repair as he pushed off like an Olympic lap-swimmer going for the gold. Instead of a pool, however, he dived into Bart's bulky two-hundred-and-fifty-pound frame, hoping to subdue the man without having to fire a shot that might alert others to their presence.

As Bart and Gadgets wrestled on the floor, the other men piled out of the van. Jorges Blancanales dashed out into the open with his Winchester and shouted for the two illegal aliens to run. The Mexicans had already been deliberating just such a course of action, and they didn't need a second invitation. Pol's father then took up position behind the Econoline, keeping his eye on Lyons, who was on his way up an outdoor stairway alongside the building that led to the second floor. The Ironman's .45 was still holstered, leaving both hands free for his M-16.

Bill Towers, who had quickly cased out the building's layout and told the group the action had to be on the upper level, headed out to cover the driveway. He was still in uniform, and as far as any curiosity-seekers or other arriving police were concerned, he was handling security during filming of an upcoming TV movie. If he was lucky, nobody would ask why they couldn't see any cameras or lighting equipment.

Rounding out the backup force, Pete Banfield positioned himself and his so-called Russian peashooter a few yards from Jorges, concentrating his attention on the flat roof of the rectangular building.

Although dwarfed by the long-haired welder, Gadgets easily outmatched Bart in terms of agility and concentrated power. A barnstorming right hook sent the greaser's tattooed fist pounding into Schwarz's midsection, nearly ruining his kidneys and deflating his lungs, but Gadgets absorbed the blow and countered with a flurry of close-quarters Monkey kung fu. Bart felt as if five men were coming at him all at once, and when a couple of the punches rattled his brainpan, the fight went out of him.

When Schwarz came back out of the office looking for him, Pol whispered, "There's a stairway in here!"

Gadgets joined his partner in the back stairwell. "Think anyone heard us?"

"Iffy," Blancanales said, taking advantage of his .45's special fold-down lever and enlarged trigger guard to secure a two-handed hold. Schwarz did the same, and they slowly started up the steps, eyes on the second-floor landing.

They were halfway up when the upper door slowly opened. At the last second, they held back from firing.

Two women in their early thirties stepped outside, so caught up in their own conversation that they didn't see Pol and Gadgets until they were about to start down the steps.

"My God . . ." one of them gasped at the sight of the pistols aimed their way.

"Don't hurt us," the other woman pleaded. "Please."

Schwarz and Blancanales were taken aback. What the hell was going on?

"What's up there?" Pol asked.

The first woman grabbed for the safety railing to steady herself. "It's just a processing room," she explained, a frightened tremble in her voice. "We do mail orders. Vitamins, mostly. Some cosmetics."

"There's no money," the other woman quickly added.

Schwarz was skeptical. Neither he nor Pol lowered their weapons. "Why don't you have a sign out front?"

"We just moved in."

"I think we're going to have to look for ourselves," Pol said, continuing up the steps.

"Who are you?"

"Friends of the family," Schwarz told her. "Now why don't you be nice ladies and put your hands on your heads?"

The women complied. Both were trembling, and their fear increased as the two men came closer to them and the doorway behind them. Finally, one of them lost control and screamed. Lunging forward, she tried to shove her way past Gadgets, but before she'd taken her second step the upper door swung open and a rattling of gunfire echoed throughout the stairwell. A .44 Magnum blast intended for Schwarz barely missed her as she dropped to the floor.

One of Wes Conzi's henchmen had fired the shots from a Smith & Wesson 29 competition handgun. Intended for silhouette target shooting, the weapon's formidable-looking 10⅝" barrel had prompted Conzi to buy a dozen of them for his workers, primarily as a visual deterrent to barrio thugs known to prey on employees in the industrial district. Gadgets returned fire before they determined if the .44 ammo could be as damaging to human flesh at such close quarters as to any paper target.

Three bursts from Gadgets's Colt .45 obliterated the gunsel's right kneecap, thigh and lung. He dropped his weapon and did a strange sort of break dance as he clawed at the doorway, trying to hold himself up. Blood was leaking from all three wounds.

Blancanales sprang forward, pushing the other woman to one side as more lead flew out of the upstairs room and bit small chunks out of the concrete walls of the staircase. He pressed his back against the wall immediately next to the doorway while Gadgets kept low, a few steps shy of the landing. Neither man could make a move toward their unseen assailants without blundering directly into the line of fire.

Blancanales turned to one of the cowering women beside him and demanded, "Is there a teenage girl held in there?"

Hyperventilating with fear, she shook her head vigorously from side to side, then babbled hysterically, "They made us come out. They made us . . ."

Another fusillade peppered the staircase, and Gadgets felt shrapnel sting his shoulder. He waited for the gunfire to subside, then grabbed for his communicator and flicked it into action. "Earth to Ironman," he whispered. "You're missing your cue. . . ."

BEFORE HE HAD A CHANCE to respond to Schwarz, Lyons found the action coming to him. He was at the top of the outside steps, leaning toward the second-story door, when it flew open in his face. He literally took it on the chin, and the force of the blow dazed him momentarily.

Two men burst out of the doorway, both toting long-barreled Smith & Wessons. One fled down the stairs, taking them two at a time, while the other swung his gun around and prepared to execute Lyons, who was down on his knees, still rallying his senses.

Down near the Ford van, Jorges worked the bolt action on his Winchester, making the carbine talk. His first shot flattened against the door two feet away from the man drawing a bead on Lyons. The gunman let his attention drift to see where the rifle shot had come from. A second bullet was already on the way, and it bored through his left elbow, taking out bone, tissue and cartilage, and nearly severing the arm. Screaming with pain, the man staggered away from the door and leaned against the stair railing.

Lyons, his head cleared, lurched forward, ramming the stock of his M-16 against the side of his foe's head with so much force that the man was bowled over the railing. A pile of scrap iron broke his fall, as well as his neck.

The second escapee made it as far as the bottom of the steps before making the acquaintance of the last four shots in Jorges Blancanales's magazine. Only two of the bullets found flesh, but the blast that caught him at the base of the neck proved fatal.

Lyons flashed the older man a quick gesture of thanks, then turned and charged into the firefight rocking the upstairs interior.

Schwarz and Blancanales had taken advantage of the commotion at the rear exit to scramble in through the main doorway, and they in turn covered the Ironman's entry to the fray. Having both exits covered, Able Team spread out, taking cover and making sure that none of the other men still inside the distribution room could get away.

Of the seventeen employees, five had already been eliminated, and another five had thrown themselves to the floor in the hope of surviving the siege to surrender. That left seven pornographers armed and firing at Able Team from behind workbenches, file cabinets and processing equipment. Those not ripping holes in the room with Smith & Wessons did their damage courtesy of Clayco 6 shotguns, over-under models firing 12-gauge shot.

Blancanales had dived behind a couch, and as a blast from one of the Claycos ate through the upholstery just inches from his right shoulder, he vaguely registered that it was the same piece of furniture he'd sat on while waiting for his interview with Claudette Simms down on Sunset Boulevard. He wasn't about to heighten the irony further by dying behind it, so he rolled away to the more unyielding cover of a steel storage cabinet and came up firing his .45. With so many people in such a crowded space, targets were easy to come by, and he clipped the man who'd been gunning for him as well as a second man two feet away.

Lyons had wounded one man on his way into the building, and with a raking burst of his M-16 he cut an 800-rpm swath of 5.56 mm death that chopped through stacks of porno cassettes and ventilated the armed workers behind them. The plastic cases for the cassettes clattered noisily to the floor, landing on several of the unarmed carpet-clutchers, who continually cried out for the carnage to cease. Their companions with the Claycos and Smith & Wessons weren't being quite as cooperative, however, and the onslaught continued, with the bullet-riddled facilities taking most of the damage.

DOWNSTAIRS, BART REGAINED consciousness and slowly stirred to his knees. Hearing the exchange of gunfire overhead, he crawled over to a tool cabinet near the door. He was more interested in flight, but if he got caught up in the carnage he wanted a more potent weapon than his torch. Reaching beneath the cabinet, he triggered a hidden latch that unlocked an equally secret panel behind the regular tools. Inside the recess was a folded Sterling Mark 6 carbine, already loaded with a 34-shot magazine of 9 mm parabellum. A British weapon, the Mark 6 had been won by Wes Conzi in a poker game and donated to the ground-floor defense of his distribution operation.

He unfolded the Sterling to its full thirty-five inches, all the while crouching low so he couldn't be seen through the office windows. At the doorway Bart hesitated, wary that through all the din spilling down the nearby stairwell he couldn't tell if anyone was on the lookout for him at the bottom of the steps. A few feet away he saw that the acetylene torch was still spouting a weak tongue of flame onto the concrete floor next to the Mercedes. Reaching behind him, the welder grabbed a handful of rags soiled with grease and oil. When he tossed them within range of the torch, a thick black cloud rose from the sudden fire.

Using the smoke screen for cover, Bart bolted across the clearing to Conzi's Mercedes. The key was in the ignition, and once he crawled across the passenger seat and got behind the wheel, he started the engine and shifted into reverse. The smoke was already filling the entire service bay, and he backed out blindly, foot on the accelerator.

Cobb, who himself had just regained consciousness, was rising to his feet, choking on the smoke, when the Mercedes screeched out at him. He tried to move clear, but his reflexes were too slow and the auto pounded into him at an angle, shattering his left leg and hurtling him into the cinder-block divider separating the bay entrances. Knocked out a second time, the muscular mechanic fell back to the cement.

Out on the lot, Pete Banfield had been the first to notice the billowing smoke, and when he shifted his attention from the roof to the service bay, he saw the Mercedes backing out and caught a glimpse of the long-haired man at the wheel. Swinging the PPSh-41 into play, Pete punctured the car's rear tires and then raised his line of fire so that bullets skimmed across the trunk and through the back window of the Mercedes.

Bart ducked across the passenger seat as 7.62 mm slugs put holes in the headrests above him. He was still able to keep one hand on the steering wheel, but when the Mercedes's rear end sank to the ground on its flattened wheels, he knew he wasn't going to have a chance to take advantage of the vehicle's fine German engineering and road-handling. Snatching his carbine instead, he twisted around and let loose with a volley of 9 mm parabellum at Banfield and the Mustang.

At the floor of the driveway, Bill Towers saw the shoot-out and yanked out his service revolver. Striking a two-handed firing stance, he steadied the weapon and squeezed off three shots. He might have felt that life in the Valley had made him go soft, but it hadn't affected his aim. Bart took two direct hits to the head, making a further mess of his boss's vehicle, which idled in the middle of the lot, going nowhere.

"ALL RIGHT!" one of the last three gunmen upstairs cried out, casting aside his emptied Smith & Wesson and raising his hands in surrender. "We give up!"

The other two followed suit, dropping their Clayco shotguns.

Able Team cautiously moved clear of cover, keeping their weapons at the ready. There were dead bodies to step over, including a few of those who had wanted no part of the bloodshed. The women who'd survived the initial skirmish in the stairwell returned, pale and shaking. In all, seven of Conzi's seventeen-person work force were finally on their feet and herded together in a tight circle for questioning. There was no recitation of the Miranda. Able Team was looking for answers, not evasion.

"The girl," Lyons demanded. "Where are they keeping the girl?"

"What girl?" one of the men asked.

"You know what girl!"

"We just work here!" another captive pleaded.

"Don't hurt us anymore!"

Blancanales scanned the group for familiar faces. Not finding any, he picked out the prisoner who looked the likeliest to talk. "You," he said. "Where are the people in charge of this operation? Claudette Simms, Wes Conzi, Otto Bendellan . . . where are they?"

The man in question slowly turned and pointed at the corner office, which was scarred with gunfire. The door had been blasted open, and it didn't appear that anyone was inside. "Mr. Conzi was in there with Bendellan."

"Was?"

The prisoner quickly explained. "There's a third exit that leads from there to the roof. They probably took that when the fighting started."

Schwarz was closest to the office, and he started toward the doorway with his .45 tight in his right hand. Halfway there, he was knocked off his feet by a resounding explosion that jarred the entire building. A portion of the floor gave way beside him and both smoke and flames shot up through the opening.

Lyons quickly took charge of the situation, firing a burst from his M-16 over the heads of the prisoners to make sure they didn't try to take advantage of the disruption. "Out the back way!" he commanded, motioning toward the doorway through which he had first entered the building. As the hungry flames surged up from the ground floor and fed on the furnishings and pornographic film stock, Lyons and Schwarz quickly prodded the survivors toward the back exit. Blancanales hesitated, then joined them when a wall of flame forced him to retreat from Conzi's office.

AT THE TIME of the first explosion from below, Conzi and Bendellan were already halfway up ladder rungs anchored in the wall of a narrow passageway behind Conzi's office. The porno chieftain led the way and opened a trapdoor that led to the roof. He was carrying a standard Uzi and had to set the weapon aside as he pulled himself up through the gap. Bendellan was right behind him, and he almost fell when a second blast, this one caused by the rupturing gas tank of Able Team's van, shook the building.

"Shit, did they send the whole motherfucking Army, or what?" Conzi complained as he helped Bendellan up onto the flat surface of the roof.

"I don't know," Bendellan wheezed. Physical activity had never been his forte, and the mild exertion of scaling the ladder had his lungs rattling with protest. Fear kept him from giving in to his fatigue. He looked around wildly for their next avenue of escape. "Where now?"

"This way!" Conzi ran to a point at the far end of the roof, where he could see the train tracks that ran through the heart of Canoga Park's industrial sector. To reach the rails they would have to jump down fifteen feet to the roof of an adjacent one-story building and then clear a barb-tipped cyclone fence separating the industrial park from the train bed.

"Hell, I can't make that jump," Bendellan said once he caught up with Conzi.

A third explosion shook the roof, forcing both men to their knees. Otto crawled away from the edge, his face chalky with fear.

"You're afraid of heights?" Conzi guessed. "Well, ain't that just fucking great! You're on your own...."

"No, wait!" Bendellan grabbed for Conzi.

The mobster rammed the Uzi's four-and-a-half-inch barrel into Bendellan's cheeks and warned him, "Get your hands off me, flake!"

Panicked, Otto shifted his grip and tried to get his hands on Conzi's weapon. The Uzi went off, scrambling Bendellan's brains with a not-so-delicate seasoning of 9 mm parabellum. Otto's body fell away from Conzi, who stuck his Uzi inside the waist of his pants and then crawled over the edge of the roof, hanging to the peripheral copings by his fingertips as he prepared to jump.

"Freeze, Conzi!"

The pornographer dangled from the rooftop as he glanced over his shoulder and saw Pol Blancanales looking up at him from the alley below.

"I want Claudette Simms!" Pol demanded. "Where is she?"

"What do I look like, an escort service?" Conzi called down. "Lemme get down and call my lawyer!"

Blancanales took aim with his .45 and ate away the coping three inches from Conzi's left hand. "Claudette Simms," Pol shouted in the wake of the gun's echo. "She's got my sister. Where?"

"I don't know."

Pol shifted his aim to the right and fired again. Conzi screamed with pain as a bullet slammed through his hand, forcing him to lose his grip and plummet to the next building. Overhead, smoke was rolling across the roof and spilling down the sides of his complex.

Groaning with pain, the pornographer dragged himself over to where his Uzi had fallen. He felt as if both his ankles were broken, and he didn't even dare look at his bullet-mangled hand, but at least he was out of Blancanales's line of vision.

"You've got nowhere to go," Pol shouted up at him. "I know Simms has a place in the Rockies. Tell me where and it might go easy for you."

Yeah, sure, Conzi thought to himself. Whoever these guys were, they weren't official. No reading of the rights, no chance to bring in attorneys to smooth things over. Their idea of going easy on him probably meant a quick bullet to the brain instead of slow torture. Fuck that shit. Conzi was sure he'd wriggle out of this mess and earn a real name for himself. Getaway Conzi. Wes the Eel. Slippery Wes.

With the Uzi in one hand, Conzi slowly rose to his knees, taking care to keep himself out of view. He groped for a loose shingle with his bloodied hand and was barely able to block out the pain and get his fingers to cooperate to close around it. He readied the Uzi in his good hand, then tossed the shingle away from him as he lunged to his feet. Here goes nothing, he thought.

Pol turned toward the sound of the shingle landing on the other side of the roof. Out of the corner of his eye, he saw Conzi rise into view and realized in a split second that he'd let himself be duped. Before he had a chance to recover, a gun fired.

It wasn't the sputtering 900-rpm chatter of an Uzi, however, but rather the death knell of a .44 Magnum bullet charging from the barrel of a Winchester rifle. Conzi's eyes widened with surprise, and he nose-dived from the roof's edge, landing with a sickening thud several yards from Blancanales.

Pol turned around and saw his father emerging from the alley with the carbine in his hands. Behind the elder Blancanales, flames continued to race out of control through the heart of Wes Conzi's multimillion-dollar empire.

"Don't tell me I never did you any favors, okay?" Jorges told his son.

23

Bill Towers had a lot of explaining to do.

When firefighters, paramedics, reporters and half the West Valley police department showed up at the burning remains of what had once been Grant's Quality Body Shop, they were somewhat skeptical that Towers had single-handedly waged an all-out war against nearly twenty opponents—especially when the casualties had been hit by at least five different types of ammunition. Since the surviving prisoners weren't going to talk until they'd had a chance to confer with their lawyers, Towers figured he had enough time to let gossip run its course. Some of the other cops were already calling him Son of Rambo. Others, more familiar with the detective's past, already suspected that somewhere in all this mess there would be evidence that pointed to the presence of one Carl Lyons. Citing the presence of hard-core pornographic materials at the scene, the media was already linking the incident to the earlier discovery of Veronica Rammite's anthrax-tainted body in Death Valley.

Able Team had appropriated Otto Bendellan's Ford Econoline and fled to Jorges Blancanales's nearby Canoga Park home after dropping off Pete Banfield. Anna was a nervous wreck, and even the sight of her husband and son walking through the door failed to calm her completely. But except for a few superficial shrapnel wounds and yet another reaggravation of Pol's problem thigh, the men had come through the firefight unscathed. Congregating in the dining room after cleaning up, they listened to the first radio reports of the shoot-out. Although they were pleased with their part in rubbing out the porno plant, their mood was far from euphoric. After all, their primary objective had not been met.

"We still don't know where they're keeping Maria," Pol said, putting their thoughts into words. "Or if she's even alive."

He hadn't intended for his mother to overhear, but when she began to sob in the kitchen he knew she had. Jorges excused himself and went to comfort her.

"What now?" Schwarz wondered aloud.

"I'll give the Farm a ring and see if they've come up with anything," Lyons said.

Pol pointed out the phone to him, then started pacing the dining room. There were framed photographs of the Blancanales children on the wall, and the sight of Maria's smiling face cut deeply. His own picture, taken for his high school graduation, struck him equally hard. He was much thinner then, with a full head of dark brown hair and the cocky smile of a street-smart kid who had all the answers. It was funny that as he got older more questions than answers cropped up, taxing his once-certain omniscience. Now, having had so many opportunities to witness the incomprehensible evils that lurked throughout the world, he was only too painfully aware that he didn't know it all. Not by a long shot.

The doorbell rang.

Pol motioned for Schwarz and Lyons to stay put while he answered it. On the way to the front door, he took out his Government .45. He wished he hadn't brought the war so close to home, but it was too late for hindsight. Precautions had to be taken.

Standing on the front porch was Bill Towers. Blancanales quickly let him in.

"Glad to see you guys got here okay," the detective said. "Quite a zoo back there."

"We've heard," Pol told him.

"I've got one of those good-news-bad-news reports," Towers said as he joined the others in the dining room.

"Good first," Pol said.

Towers sat down and wiped soot from his forehead. "We went through the rubble looking for evidence, and we found a few cassettes still intact," he expressed.

"And...?"

"They were in Conzi's office, along with a few scribbled notes. From what we can make out, Pol, it looks like your sister's still alive."

Pol's eyes lit up. "Yeah?"

"That's also the bad news," Towers said. He looked around. "Your folks around?"

"In the backyard," Pol told him.

Towers still lowered his voice. "Apparently just before we hit the place, Conzi and Bendellan were watching the tapes and making notes...stuff to cut out, editing marks, things like that. They'd already watched footage of your sister's friend and that Felsur girl being snuffed—"

"Scum," Pol spat, pounding his fist on the table.

"The tape in the VCR was of Maria," Towers went on. "I'm not going to go into detail, because it's pretty hard stuff. From the looks of it, they've got her on some kind of drug and—"

Blancanales interrupted again, this time with a string of Spanish profanities that would have made his father blush. When he was through, he calmed himself and reverted back to English, asking Towers, "How can you tell she's alive?"

"Like I said, we can't be sure. But in the notes there was mention of other scenes they wanted to use her for. And in one margin Conzi had scrawled 'Keep her around,' so there's room for hope."

"If we can get to her in time," Pol said. "Was there anything about where they've got her?"

Towers sighed and shook his head. "*Nada*. Our best bet there is that we found a hotel key in Bendellan's pocket and traced it to a hotel on the other side of the Valley. Picked up a guy sleeping there, but he's not talking. The D.A. might dangle a carrot to see if he bites, but that could take hours, maybe days."

"Hell!" Pol shouted in frustration. "Put me alone in a room with him and I'll get him to talk!"

"Probably," Towers agreed. "But it'll never happen."

Lyons came in from the other room, an enigmatic expression on his face.

"Come up with anything?" Schwarz asked him.

Lyons nodded. "Brognola says the government's going to meet Fabyan's terms."

Schwarz was incredulous. "You're kidding! Let those mob bosses go? Hell, it'll never work. Never in a million years."

Even though he knew a successful trade-off would lead to the release of his sister, Pol was equally skeptical. "Fabyan won't hold up his end of the bargain."

"Probably not," Lyons agreed.

"Did you try to talk some sense into them?"

"Yeah," the Ironman replied, taking a seat at the table. "But they're still going through with it . . . sort of."

"What do you mean 'sort of'?" Schwarz asked.

Lyons slowly let a grin fill his face. "Well, guys, it's like this . . ."

THE DAWN SKY WAS just beginning to brighten over the barren flatlands of Oldham County, Texas. For miles in all directions, parched desert sand sprawled out toward the horizon. Here and there a round clump of tumbleweed stirred in the slight breeze, and an occasional roadrunner sprinted across the terrain in search of a small lizard or other snack to start its day off right.

Then a cloud of dust rose in the distance, marking the approach of a new station wagon. The vehicle was following no road, and tracks from its radial tires left deep, clear impressions in the hardpan. At a spot that qualified as a candidate for the nation's official Middle of Nowhere, the car came to a stop. Four men got out of the back seat and stretched their limbs. They were well into middle age, and the baggy suits they were wearing had a prison-issue look to them.

Two armed police officers emerged from the front seat and circled around to open the rear tailgate. One of them pulled out a large beach umbrella and four lightweight folding chairs. The other officer withdrew a Coleman ice chest from the station wagon and followed his cohort to a spot near the other men. The umbrella was opened and stabbed into the sandy soil so that it would shield the four men in suits from the rising sun's rays. The men calmly sat down in the chairs, no words were spoken.

Their job completed, the two officers got back into the station wagon and drove off, retracing the southbound trail they'd made in the sand. In less than a half hour they would reach the nearest official roadway, U.S. Interstate 40, more popularly known as Route 66.

Alone in the desert, the four men poured themselves cold drinks as they watched the sun rise. The temperature slowly began to rise along with it.

Ten minutes passed.

Twenty.

Then, off in the distance, a black speck crept out of the sun and eventually took the shape of a Beechcraft Bonanza A36TC aircraft. The airplane dipped low as it came in over the desert, and the four men rose from their chairs and stepped clear of the umbrella so that they could be seen from above. They waved to the pilot as the six-seater flew past them, lowering its landing gear.

After touching down on the tarmac a quarter mile away, the single-engine craft circled around and came to a stop near the four men, who left behind the umbrella and chairs and carried only the ice chest to the plane.

Sam, Claudette Simms's cameraman, was at the controls of the Beechcraft, and Rudy moved from the copilot's seat to open the plane's door and let down the steps. Hardened as he was, the thug couldn't help but feel a sense of awe as he watched the four passengers board. After all, here were perhaps the four most powerful men in the Midwest, corporation heads and politicians notwithstanding. The bosses. The dons.

"Welcome aboard," Rudy told the men, taking care to show his respect by bowing slightly as each man moved past him and into the plane. He thought he recognized Pete Cinzo of Cleveland and Joe Debbs of Chicago, who carried the ice chest. "You can leave that cooler behind. We have champagne aboard. And caviar and—"

Rudy stopped talking when he found the tip of a Government Model .45 pressed against the knot of his tie.

"I think we'll take it, okay?" Joe Debbs told him.

Before Sam realized that something was amiss, another of the men put a second Colt within inches of his skull and suggested, "Let me take the controls and you won't have to kiss my ring."

Without taking his eyes off the .45, Sam eased out of the pilot's seat. The man with the gun took his place and checked a clipboard dangling from the control panel. He grinned as he flipped through the pages. "Directions. How thoughtful."

Sam took a better look at the men who had taken over the plane. Up this close, the makeup and wigs were far less convincing than they had been from several hundred feet up.

"Who are you guys?" he asked.

"Smile," Gadgets Schwarz told him. "You're on *Candid Camera*."

24

The plan had been Brognola's, inspired in part by Blancanales's unfortunate misadventure with YouRan Productions. Hours before, while the Stony Man chief of
operations had been on the phone with Carl Lyons back in
Canoga Park, Jack Grimaldi had been making his way to
Los Angeles with recent mug shots of the syndicate dons he
and Able Team would be impersonating. Using legitimate
Hollywood connections, the four men had undergone their
transformations at the hands of Salvatore Ingres, a four-
time Oscar-winning makeup artist. It had taken three tedi-
ous hours to complete the disguises, but now, as they found
themselves in control of the syndicate Beechcraft and on
their way to Wyoming, the four commandos felt certain the
elaborate planning had been worth it.

"Now, then," Lyons spoke to Rudy and Sam as Grimaldi jockeyed the plane off their makeshift runway,
"what's Fabyan's plan for the anthrax now that he's supposedly got his bosses back?"

The two prisoners had their arms bound to their sides and
their legs strapped together so that they looked limbless, like
human snakes. Sam stared sullenly at the floor, while Rudy
met his interrogators with a head-on gaze.

"You gotta promise me I go free if I talk," he bargained.

"Oh? Is that so?"

Rudy shrugged. "Your choice, man."

"I see," Lyons responded calmly. He turned to Pol and Schwarz, who were poised on either side of the plane's doorway. On Lyons's nod, Pol opened the door. Wind rushed in, but Grimaldi was taking care to hold the plane's course low and steady enough to keep the craft stable.

Grabbing Rudy by the collar of his shirt, Lyons jerked him from his chair and dragged him to the open doorway, forcing the prisoner's head out far enough for him to see the long first step to the ground several hundred feet below.

"Hey, man, wait!" Rudy cried, terror in his voice.

"Here's the deal, pal," Lyons countered. "We'll let you free right now if you *don't* talk, okay?"

Rudy didn't have to wait long to weigh his options. "I'll talk!" he shouted. "I'll talk!"

Lyons tugged the man back into the aircraft and Pol closed the door. Grimaldi picked up speed, pushing the needle toward the 200-mph mark as he gained altitude. Once he was back in his chair, it still took Rudy a few moments to shake off his fear.

Sam sneered at his cohort. "Chickenshit!"

"Shut up!" Rudy told him.

"Yeah, listen to your buddy," Lyons told Sam. "Or maybe you want to play 'Bombs Away' in his place?"

"You can't scare me," Sam insisted.

Without warning, Gadgets leaned forward and rammed his fist into Sam's solar plexus, knocking the wind out of him. As the cameraman's mouth instinctively flew open, Lyons filled it with a wad of cloth.

"Boo," Schwarz said, using his necktie to complete the gag.

Lyons turned back to Rudy. "So, where were we?"

Rudy said, "Fabyan's giving back all but one of the missiles. They should already be at a drop-off point near Scotts Bluff. That's in Nebraska, just across the Wyoming border. We gave the green light for your people to get directions when we landed to pick you up."

"Good show," Lyons said. "Why's he keeping one of the missiles?"

"We've got a scientist who figures he can build up a new stockpile using just a portion of the anthrax," Rudy explained. "Fabyan figures the mob can peddle it overseas for top dollar. Let the maniacs kill each other with it and do us all a favor."

"What a guy," Lyons mocked. "Listen, did he ever really consider bombing a storm front?"

Rudy shrugged. "I work for Claudette, not the mob, so I don't know for sure. But I doubt it. Seems to me the syndicate's got too many friends in high places that would start backing off if Fabyan pulled something like that. Bad PR, if you know what I mean."

"Little late for that, don't you think?" Lyons said. "You already made headlines dumping that girl's body in Death Valley."

"Not to mention the fireworks at the porn plant," Schwarz added.

"Yeah, but that would all blow over in a few months." Rudy snickered cynically. "Always does. Shit, the public gets a fucking rise outta this crap anyway, and you know it. Special bulletins on the tube, gossip in the grocery lines—shakes things up, gets their blood pumping for a change."

Lyons looked at his cohorts. None of them could fully believe what they were hearing. Dozens of people had already been killed and millions more had been threatened, and this guy was carrying on like he and his buddies were performing a public service. Blancanales took over the questioning, showing Rudy a picture of his sister.

"Is this girl at the ranch?"

Rudy nodded. "Yeah. A real looker, isn't she?"

Two punches later, Rudy's lip was split and bleeding and a bruise was already forming a dark crescent under his left eye. Blancanales had his gun pointed at the man's heart.

"We're going to untie you, then you're going to draw a layout of this ranch for us," he told Rudy. "And you're going to give us a few tips on how to throw a surprise party for the folks down there, because if we don't come away with that girl still alive, you're going to die in a way that will make your snuff films look tame...understood?"

EDDIE NEVRUT HADN'T BEEN the only member of the Armed Forces who'd sought a lucrative sideline as a supplier of stolen military weapons to Dave X. Fabyan and other syndicate contacts. Closer to the Rockies, the mob had cultivated links with several supply officers at the Fort Carson Military Reserve in Colorado Springs. It was through these connections that Fabyan was able to give Kenneth Shanks a number of weapons systems to consider in the mob's newfound plan to export the possibilities of anthrax warfare.

Although Shanks was first and foremost a scientist, during his forty-year stint at Midwest Research he'd pored over enough schematic designs and prototypes to be proficient in evaluating weapons. Apprised of Fabyan's long-range plans for the anthrax and having a deep-seated hatred of the people of the Third World who would become the primary victims, Shanks eagerly threw himself into the task of trying to determine the most feasible weapons package to combine the contaminant with.

He quickly eliminated any redesigning of missiles like the Copperhead or overall systems like the HAWK and Chaparral. They would be too expensive, too bulky, and difficult to secure in large quantities. The logistics of arms smuggling required a weapon with far greater portability and less technological sophistication.

Light Antitank Weapons and LAWs descendants like the Dragon and Viper were briefly considered, since their size was ideal and the relative simplicity of their designs lent itself to easy modification of ammunition and firing mechanisms. But it was decided that a longer-ranged weapon was needed. After all, even the Dragon's 1000-km range would burst an anthrax charge too close to those who had fired it, particularly if there was a head wind.

That left one final alternative in Shanks's mind, and when Claudette Simms and Fabyan entered yet another of the film rooms the scientist had appropriated for his duties, they found Shanks madly scribbling notes on a weapon blueprint laid out on a drafting table.

"Yes!" Shanks exclaimed, racing his pencil with a flourish across the paper. "This will work perfectly!"

"What's that?" Fabyan asked.

"The Stinger." Shanks swiveled around in his chair and pointed to the blueprints, which were laid out on a long oak credenza on the other side of the room.

A shoulder-fired tublike weapon, the Stinger lived up to its appropriate name. It was equipped with an infrared homing missile capable of locking a fix on the heat emitted by enemy aircraft and striking its target propelled by a main engine that kicked in after initial firing from a small launch motor housed in the main body of the weapon.

"You're sure it would work?" Claudette asked.

"Almost positive," the scientist responded. He moved over to the credenza and pointed at various parts of the bazooka-shaped weapon. As he explained, a thin whitish film gathered at the corners of his mouth, and he almost spit the words in his excitement. "It's no problem to rig the warhead with an anthrax charge, and we all know the Stinger can hold up on the battlefield until it's used. All you have to do is sight an enemy plane heading back to native soil and shoot it down. The anthrax will spread on the way down...and if there are clouds, you could come up with the same results you were threatening the Feds with.''

Claudette nodded, following the scientist's train of thought. She could sense that Fabyan was infected by Shanks's presentation and was secretly thrilled. This had been her idea, and they all knew it. It was the start of more than a mere cherry deal for the mob. It was also shaping up to be a long-sought ticket into that criminal organization for her. Granted, the mob was an essentially chauvinistic organization with no record of a woman ever having risen to a position of recognized power. But times were changing, and there would likely be a first—soon. If so, Claudette was going to make sure the honor came to her. She'd already laid the groundwork. No one who had witnessed one of her smut films would ever dare accuse her of being weak-kneed or afraid of the violence that was a mobster's inevitable stock-in-trade.

''The Stinger's more complicated than these other weapons, isn't it?'' she said, pointing to the blueprints of the other antitank weapons. ''Isn't that something to consider?''

''Not really,'' Shanks maintained. ''Even a moron could use the Stinger after a little training. The Afghans know how to work it already.... Hell, they've damn near chased the Russians back home with 'em.''

''I remember reading that,'' Claudette recalled. She turned to Fabyan. ''Any trouble getting ahold of them?''

''So-so,'' Fabyan said. ''Since they broke up that smuggling ring back East that was running them down to Central America, security's way up.''

''Well, you got this one, right?'' Shanks said hopefully.

Fabyan nodded. ''Yeah, but we're gonna want dozens, maybe hundreds. Redeyes would be easier.''

''Pah! The Redeye's a piece of shit compared to the Stinger!'' Shanks removed a handkerchief from his pocket and dabbed the foam from his lips, patting the missile on the credenza as if it were a loyal pet. "I say this is the way to go!"

"Then we'll take a good look at it," Fabyan promised. Out of the corner of his eye, he saw one of his men standing in the doorway.

"We've made radio contact with the Beechcraft," the man told his boss. "You wanna talk to 'em?"

Fabyan nodded. He lightly put his hand on Shanks's shoulder and gave him a reassuring pat. "Good work, Doc. Keep it up!"

Shanks nodded. "Thanks, but I think I need to take a break." The telltale gleam came to his eyes. "I was wondering, that Mexican girl..."

Claudette could take a hint. She told the scientist, "'I think she's rested up. Why don't I take you to her?"

"That would be nice," Shanks said, sticking the foam-flecked handkerchief in his pocket.

DURING THOSE HOURS when Jack Grimaldi and Able Team had undergone the makeup transformation that had enabled them to succeed in the first part of their so-called Operation Anthrax, Gadgets Schwarz had put the time to good use. A man well-known for his vocal dexterity, Schwarz had listened carefully to tape recordings of the four mafia bosses they would be impersonating, and by the time he'd been turned into a would-be clone of Chi-town's Joe Debbs, Gadgets had mastered not only Debbs's heavy Midwestern drawl but also the speech patterns of the three other men. Similarly, he'd studied Rudy's voice during the thug's interrogation.

When the Beechcraft Bonanza cleared the Continental Divide and began closing in on their final destination, Schwarz moved up to the copilot's seat, preparing for the inevitable moment of radio contact with Claudette Simms's ranch. He didn't have long to wait. The call came less than two minutes later.

"Mountain Goat to Sparrowhawk. Do you read? Over."

"Roger, Mountain Goat," Schwarz reported, drawing out the words slightly and speaking in a lower, slower voice than usual. "Sparrowhawk coming back to the nest with four early worms. Over."

To help mask his voice further, Schwarz put his electronic wizardry to work and tampered with the radio controls so that a constant crackle of static marred the transmission. When the radio operator down at the ranch reported the static, Schwarz passed it off as atmospheric disturbance and nothing to be overly concerned about.

"Hey, Rudy," Dave X. Fabyan's voice suddenly came over the radio. "How about if you put Cinzo on the horn? Over."

"No can do," Schwarz said after a pause, continuing to speak in Rudy's voice. "Mr. Cinzo's napping and said he didn't want to be disturbed until we reached the ranch." Despite all the preparatory work he'd put into learning how to imitate the gangsters, Schwarz wasn't anxious to do any more impersonations than were absolutely necessary. With that in mind, he quickly added, "Sam just checked and they're all still dozing. Apparently with all the transfers they didn't get much sleep. Over."

"Well, shit," Fabyan was heard to say. "Hey, what's with all the fucking static, anyway?"

"Not sure. Over."

"Look, you'll be here in a few minutes, so the guys are gonna have to get up anyway, right?" Even through the crackling, Schwarz could detect suspicion in Fabyan's voice. He wasn't buying the nap bit. "No offense, Rudy, but we aren't gonna let you land until I hear personally from one of the bosses. Preferably Cinzo. Got that? Over."

Schwarz paused to trade glances with Grimaldi, who was going over the navigational charts. The pilot whispered, "I don't see any other place besides their airstrip to bring it down on. Better humor him."

"Affirmative," Schwarz reported to Fabyan. "I'll give a wake-up call and have someone get back to you. Over and out."

Keying off the radio, Schwarz left his copilot's seat and joined the passengers. "Which of the bosses does Fabyan know the least?" he asked the real Rudy.

Rudy shrugged. "Hey, I work mostly for the lady, remember? I don't deal with Fabyan that much."

"Guess."

Rudy thought it over. "Well, Cinzo's never really gotten along with Chicago, so I'd say Debbs."

"Good," Schwarz said, lightly touching his makeup. "I'm already in character, then."

One of the items Able Team had brought along in the ice chest was a tape player with voice samples of each chieftain. Schwarz cued up Debbs and slipped on the player's lightweight headphones as he returned to the pilot's cabin. While he listened, Gadgets took a deep breath and glanced out at the scenery. Grimaldi had just brought them out of a cloud bank, and they were passing over the snowy peaks of the Grand Tetons Cathedral Group and circling back toward the Wind River range. Armies of tall pines rose up through the snow, and in the lower elevations a few hardy blossoms lent color to the landscape. It seemed almost incomprehensible to Schwarz that this pristine wilderness could be the haven of such a despicable pack of jackals as Fabyan, Simms and the Chicago mobster whose taped voice was coming over his headphones. The voice was filled with lawless vitality and the arrogance of unchecked power.

"Coming up on the ranch," Grimaldi announced, pointing out a clearing in the distance. "I'm going to pass over once to get a bead on the airstrip. You better start sweet-talking.''

Schwarz nodded and switched off the tape player, trading one set of headphones for another. He eyed the layout of Simms's ranch as he put the call through to whoever was handling dispatches for Fabyan.

"Sparrowhawk to Mountain Goat. Over." Gadgets was still speaking in Rudy's voice. Being in sight of the ranch, he had no choice but to ease off on the static he'd imposed on the transmission. It was going to be hard enough easing suspicions without continuing to pass off flimsy excuses about poor reception.

"Mountain Goat to Sparrowhawk. We read you."

Gadgets said, "I've got Joe Debbs here."

After a break on the other line, Fabyan's voice came on. "Welcome back to the real world, Mr. Debbs."

Schwarz altered his voice to impersonate the Chicago mafioso. "You call this the real world? I don't see no fucking skyscrapers."

"We'll get you back to Chicago soon enough."

"Good. Meantime, I hope you got some extra clothes down there," Schwarz said. "We got our fucking prison suits on, and I don't want to freeze my fucking ass off when I get off the plane."

"Not to worry, sir. Let me speak to Mr. Conzi, okay?"

"He's in the head. Prison food didn't agree with him." There was a pause. Schwarz exhaled lightly. Was Fabyan buying it? He hoped so. "You can talk to him when we're down there, okay?"

"Okay," Fabyan said. "Hey, by the way, your cousin Tommy called me a couple days ago, says the family's gonna treat you to a real whoop-de-do."

Schwarz imitated a belly laugh he'd heard on the tape of Joe Debbs. "Well, I should fucking hope so! Look, Fabyan, I gotta get back and strap in for landing. Over."

Grimaldi had taken the Beechcraft over the ranch's airstrip and was banking for the approach. Schwarz could see a few sentries stationed at various high points on the sprawling property. He was reaching to switch off the radio when one last communication came over the speaker.

"I don't know who the fuck you are up there," Fabyan said, "but Joe Debbs doesn't have a cousin Tommy."

Schwarz looked at Grimaldi. Trap time. There really wasn't much choice but to ride the bluff out. Staying in character, Gadgets retorted, "Says who? What the fuck do you know about my family tree, shit-for-brains?"

Carl Lyons rushed in from the passenger compartment, a look of alarm in his eyes. Interrupting Schwarz, he shouted, "Forget the charade! Somebody down there just hauled out a Stinger! They get off a clean shot and we're dead meat!"

25

Sergeant Rip Gish was the man with the Stinger. He'd brought it up to Simms's ranch from Colorado Springs the day before, along with the other weapons Fabyan had requested on behalf of Kenneth Shanks. Two partners in his smuggling operation had come along, and they'd also been pressed into duty as last-second additions to the ranch security force. None of the three men had wanted to get directly involved in Fabyan's mob affairs, but they needed only a quick reminder that one anonymous phone call could line them up for courts-martial. At least for the time being, it was in their best interests to follow the *caporegime's* orders as if they were his *soldati* and not those of the United States Armed Forces.

While his cohorts raced out to guard the perimeter, Gish slung the Stinger onto his shoulder and quickly swept the viewfinder across the cloudy sky until the Beechcraft fell into its sights and the missile's homing system signaled that it had a lock on the aircraft. Since the warhead wasn't one of the yet-to-be-developed anthrax carriers, he didn't have to worry about bringing the craft down too close to the ranch.

"Go sic 'em, boy," Gish whispered as he braced himself and triggered the Stinger's launch motor. There was only a mild recoil considering the dimensions of the weapon, and by the time he'd lowered the firing tube, Gish could see the missile's primary engine kick in and begin thrusting the warhead toward its heat-emitting target. Although the Beechcraft had just banked sharply and was turning away from the ranch, Gish knew the diversionary tactics would be of little use. The Beechcraft was done for.

Sure enough, less than fifteen seconds later, the six-man Bonanza took a direct hit to its midsection and erupted into a blazing fireball. Although a few large sections of fuselage and most of one wing broke away in some recognizable shape, most of the plane showered down on the pines as small, hopelessly mangled bits of twisted metal. Gish couldn't see any falling bodies in all the smoke and flame, but he was sure that those aboard the craft had been shredded by the Stinger's destructive force.

An impressive demonstration of the weapon, if he had to say so himself.

But wait.

He could see bodies after all.

One...two...three...four bodies, all of them intact, coming down from the sky.

And then he saw parachutes shoot up from the men's backpacks and fill out like mushroom caps, jerking them up momentarily before slowing their rate of descent.

"Shit!" Gish swore, casting aside the Stinger's firing tube and homing equipment. Whoever those bastards were, he knew he'd damn well better track them down and finish off the job he started. From his belt holster he withdrew an Army-issue Beretta 92SB-F, and as he bolted across the ranch grounds toward the wooded area, he switched off the safety. He was going to meet the enemy on the run and firing.

ABLE TEAM AND GRIMALDI LEAPED from the Beechcraft mere seconds before it was downed by the blast that sent Rudy and Sam to their deaths. The men had jumped from a dangerously low altitude, but when fiery shrapnel from the remains of the plane fell on their parachutes, burning holes in the taut nylon, their descent became even more swift and perilous.

"My leg's not gonna like this," Blancanales muttered to himself as he tugged on the shroud lines to veer wide of the trees. Like the other men, he'd raided the ice chest for an Uzi submachine gun and a three-clip of 40 mm grenades to supplement his holstered .45, and the extra weight wasn't helping matters—not that he was complaining. A paratroop raid on the ranch hadn't been one of their options, and knowing they would have to ad-lib their assault made him grateful for all the artillery they could muster.

He was also grateful for the jump school experience during his Nam years. As the ground rushed up to meet him, Pol was able to twist his lines just enough to guide himself into a drifting snowbank that provided more than four feet of loose powder to break his fall. His wounded thigh still let him know it didn't approve of skydiving as a means of therapy, but at least he could walk after he'd severed himself from the lines.

More than a hundred yards off to his right, the remains of the decimated Beechcraft crashed into the woods. Thick smoke began to roll out between the trees. Blancanales saw Lyons and Grimaldi land between him and the wreckage. In both cases the men executed picture-perfect rolls the moment they hit the ground. Their chutes collapsed immediately around them which meant they were able to get out of their harnesses quickly and dash to the cover of a nearby stone fence before Gish and one of his partners began firing at them.

SCHWARZ HAD BEEN BLOWN wide of the clearing, and after crashing through the upper limbs of an ancient cottonwood he found himself dangling eight feet above ground. He was bleeding through his makeup face from several facial scratches.

"Wonderful," he chided himself, grappling with his harness. "Hell, Hermann, your mother could come down better than that!"

Preoccupied with freeing himself, Gadgets didn't notice one of Gish's partners stealing through the woods toward him, clutching his service Beretta. However as the gunman dropped into a firing crouch and raised his weapon, a streak of sunlight coming through the cottonwoods glanced off the metallic frames of his glasses. Schwarz noted the glint and looked up, spotting the man less than thirty yards away. He was only halfway out of the harness, and there was no time for him to reach for any of his weapons. He felt like a fly trapped in a web, looking at the spider who'd built it.

Then again, most flies weren't athletically inclined or skilled in acrobatics. Using the taut shroud lines for leverage, Gadgets torqued his body sharply, kicking up his feet so he was positioned parallel to the ground and therefore a smaller target for the 9 mm parabellum blasts that came hurtling toward him, splintering twigs and nicking one of his lines.

His momentum had carried him back near the trunk of the tree, and he kicked off with both feet, swinging clear of the assailant's second volley. Freeing one hand long enough to unfasten the last clip on his harness, Schwarz was disconnected from the shroud lines, and when he let go he went tumbling to the forest floor. He somersaulted expertly and bounced to his feet. The maneuver took the other man by surprise, buying Gadgets enough time to yank out his Government Model. The .45 was set on its potent three-shot function, and when he fired, thunder roared through the woods and the other gunman was knocked backward by the death bursts. His Beretta fired wildly into the snow until the clip was empty, but he was already dead, and when his legs got the message he crumpled into the snow.

Schwarz didn't waste time checking the body. He quickly reloaded his .45, then slipped it back in its holster, deciding to go with the Uzi as he began to creep through the woods toward the clearing where he heard his comrades caught up in another firefight.

"ENOUGH OF THIS SHIT!" Lyons groused as he ducked another round of fire from Gish and the third soldier from Colorado Springs. "We can't spend all day trapped out here."

Grimaldi was next to him behind the stone fence. He bobbed up long enough to get off a few rounds with his Uzi and to place the enemy. "They're behind a mound about fifty yards away. Six o'clock." He grabbed for his three-pack of grenades. "I say we give 'em a Fourth of July finale."

Lyons nodded, separating his own 40 mm pineapples. "You go left, I go right. On three," he told Grimaldi.

The men counted off in unison, then let fly with the grenades, throwing them one after the other, trying to vary the angle and distance so that they would do the greatest possible damage. Readying their Uzis, they waited for the first charge to detonate. Then they bounded over the fence and zigzagged toward the mound, ducking their heads low to avoid flying shrapnel.

Gish and his partner were likewise distracted by the explosions surrounding them, and when they hunched over and covered their heads as snow, gravel and frag pelted the mound, they were in no position to defend themselves against the two-man assault force that charged into their midst. Although they tried to bring their Berettas into play, it was too late. Uzi death-chatter was the last thing they heard before 9 mm fire dug into them with lethal abandon.

The slain soldiers were out of uniform, but as he checked the bodies for pulses, Lyons noted Gish's dog tags. "Hell, this guy's a goddamn Army sergeant."

"He obviously switched armies," Schwarz said.

Lyons and Grimaldi were prying off facial putty and using snow to wash off some of their makeup when Schwarz and Blancanales entered the clearing and joined them.

"One of those grenades nearly took me out, but good work anyway," Schwarz said, dabbing blood from his face with his sleeve. "And no wisecracks about my landing. I had holes in my chute the size of basketball hoops."

"Excuses, excuses," Grimaldi teased.

Lyons pointed to a tendril of smoke curling above the tree line several hundred yards away. "Well, we sure as hell don't have any element of surprise left. We've got no choice but to storm the place. Let's pick directions and fan out. I'll go north."

"South," Grimaldi ventured.

"East," said Schwarz.

"Good," Blancanales said. The western approach was the quickest, and he wanted to be the first one to reach the ranch.

26

Dave X. Fabyan was standing near the corral, looking toward the smoke and flames that indicated the final resting spot of the downed aircraft. He could also see the crater-scarred clearing where Gish and the other soldier had fallen.

"I don't know what the hell kinda goddamn army they got out there," he cursed under his breath, "but I ain't waitin' around to find out!"

While Claudette Simms's dwindling security force staked out a tightened perimeter around the barn and ranch house, the *caporegime* strode purposefully to the muddied driveway and slipped behind the wheel of the Range Rover Gish and his cohorts had driven up from Colorado Springs. Fabyan owned the vehicle and had a spare set of keys. He started the ignition and spun a fantail of slush into the air as he sped away from the ranch.

The main road clung precariously to the side of White Mountain, with only a modestly reinforced guardrail separating the shoulder from a precipitous plunge to the rocky slope below. Fabyan knew that the chances of there being oncoming traffic in the opposite lane was remote, so he stayed close to the mountain and kept up his speed, glad that most of the recent snow had melted. With any luck he could get to the highway without incident and then speed south to the airfield near Jackson Hole. From there he'd get his ass back to Cleveland and lie low until this whole sorry fiasco blew over. Claudette's scheme had its merits, but there were other ways to make his way up the organizational ladder. Especially since it looked like Cinzo, Debbs and the others were still on ice. And if he did things his way, he wouldn't have to cut Simms in on the action. He didn't trust her for a second. He knew her type. Give her a chance and she'd screw you every which way but loose. Pushy broad thought she could smile and shake her booty a few times and he'd roll over and play stepping-stone. Fat chance. He'd gotten this far on his own, and he'd go it alone once things had cooled off. Yeah, lie low now, then come out on top. That was the way to do it.

Cornering around a bend in the road, Fabyan eased off on the accelerator and veered into the right lane, avoiding a small rock slide that had spilled out onto the road. Then, up ahead, he spotted a man climbing up over the railing onto the road, Uzi in hand.

"Oh, no, you don't," Fabyan seethed, pressing on the accelerator.

GADGETS HAD JUST CLIMBED down from the railing when he saw the Range Rover barreling toward him. He didn't have to waste time trying to recognize the driver to know that the man behind the wheel was interested in a bit of lethal hit-and-run. He promptly threw himself across the roadway, bounding into the westbound lane just as Fabyan rushed by, catching Schwarz's right ankle with the front fender.

Schwarz landed hard on the asphalt but rolled on contact and came up into a crouch, still holding the Uzi. He sprayed what was left in his magazine at the underside of the vehicle, taking out three of its four tires. The Ranger immediately lurched out of control, with its rear end swerving sharply to the left, caroming off the railing and sending the vehicle off in the other direction.

Fabyan wrestled with the steering wheel, but his getaway vehicle was acting as if it had a mind of its own. After bounding up the slope of the mountain next to the westbound lane, the Range Rover zagged one final time and plowed through the railing on the other side. The wagon looked for a moment as if it was going to stay lodged between sections of the barrier, but when Fabyan tried to struggle out of the vehicle, he only succeeded in rocking it free.

Schwarz could hear the man's screams as the car dipped over the precipice. Moments later there was the sickening crunch of metal smashing into jagged rock. Then an explosion rocked the otherwise tranquil scenery.

Gadgets lingered at the railing long enough to see flames engulf Fabyan's makeshift pyre; then he started up the road toward the ranch. His ankle felt as if it had already swollen one size larger than his boot, but he could still walk on it. There would be time to rest later.

KENNETH SHANKS COULDN'T figure out what the hell was going on. He hadn't been told about the pending arrival of the mob bosses, and when explosions and gunfire began to sound from one end of the ranch property to the other, he was terrified.

Jumping up from the bed where Maria Blancanales lay in a semistupor induced by Seconal and Quaaludes, the scientist nervously pulled on his jockey shorts and moved toward the window. Peering through the curtains, he saw two ranch guards crouched behind an ancient, rusting buckboard, firing at a third man lying near an old well more than forty yards away. The man by the well threw something, and seconds later the buckboard and the two guards near it were torn to bits by a violent explosion that also shattered the window Shanks was standing in front of.

Shards of flying glass cut the man in several places, and he screamed as he spun away from the window.

"My eyes!" he cried out, covering his face with his hands. "I can't see!"

"Shut up, you old fool!" Claudette Simms snapped as she rushed into the room carrying a small AMT autopistol.

"I'm blind!" Shanks continued to moan. Blood flowed between the fingers he held over his eyes.

Claudette stepped over and stuck the two-and-a-half-inch barrel in the bare flab of the scientist's midsection. "Keep it up and you're going to be *dead*, too!"

"You have to help me!"

"Forget it, old man!" Claudette leaned her shoulder into the man, knocking him off balance. She shoved him again, this time so hard that he tumbled out the window he'd been standing before earlier. They were on the ground floor, so he only fell a few feet, but a jagged edge of the broken glass severed an artery in his neck and his blood spurted over the snowy ground.

Claudette turned away from the window and grabbed Maria by the arm. The younger woman hadn't been touched by Shanks and was still wearing a cotton nightgown. There was fear in her eyes, but Maria was too sedated to resist as the other woman pulled her to her feet.

"You're my ticket out of here, princess," Claudette whispered in Maria's ear as they started for the doorway. "Come on . . ."

"Let her go!"

Claudette wheeled around, holding Maria in front of her. Silhouetted in the frame of the window Shanks had just fallen through was another man. As he climbed into the room, Claudette recognized the intruder through the smeared makeup.

"Let her go!" Pol Blancanales repeated. He had his Uzi pointed at Claudette.

The pornographer squeezed farther behind Maria and pointed her AMT at Maria's head. "She'll die before I do!"

"Let her go," Pol repeated a third time.

"Only after you let *me* go," Claudette bartered.

"You used me," Pol said, his voice cold. "You've killed two innocent girls...and God knows how many others. Do you really think I'd let you go free?"

"Spare me the sermon. I'm offering you a simple trade," Claudette replied. "Her for me."

Pol was in a quandary. One wrong move and Maria was dead. And yet he knew that if Claudette went free . . .

His answer came when he saw the doped expression fade from his sister's face. She glanced knowingly at her brother, then suddenly let her legs give out beneath her. She dropped a few inches before Claudette could get a firm grip on her. Those few inches were all Pol needed. Given a target, he squeezed off one shot from his Uzi.

The bullet went in just above Claudette's right eye, shattering the socket bone and ripping through brain before exiting through the back of her skull. She loosened her grip on Maria and slumped backward, dropping her handgun. Bouncing off the foot of the bed, the woman fell on top of several porno magazines Kenneth Shanks had been flipping through prior to climbing into bed with Maria. Her blood flowed across the glossy pages.

"Oh, Rosario!"

"There, there," Pol said, stepping forward and embracing his sister. "It's going to be okay. It's all over...."

As the two siblings held on to one another, the sounds of gunfire abated outside the ranch house. Moments later, Carl Lyons peered in the broken window and called out to Pol, "Everything all right in there?"

"Yeah," Blancanales said, feeling his sister's tears against his cheek. "Yeah..."

EPILOGUE

The same night he received the news that Claudette Simms and Dave X. Fabyan had met their deaths during the raid on the Wyoming ranch, Nash Felsur died peacefully in his sleep at the high-security compound he was sharing with his wife in the basement of the Justice Department. Mrs. Julia Felsur took advantage of the government's witness relocation program and is living under an assumed name somewhere in the continental United States.

With convicted syndicate bosses Cinzo, Debbs, Altorre, and Schatzeder still behind bars, organized crime in the Midwest is reportedly going through a period of transition, with underbosses and *caporegimes* taking stock of their families. Although incidences of mob crime have decreased, and are in most cases directed against rival families jockeying for position, no one on either side of the law is predicting that the Cosa Nostra has been put out of circulation.

Still recuperating from injuries sustained in the shoot-out on Hamstead Road, operative Lao Ti has been granted an indefinite leave of absence from her duties at Stony Man Farm. She is currently in Taiwan, living with her mother and sister. She has already been contacted by the State Department with an offer to accept a position with the American embassy in Taipei and is expected to give an answer shortly.

Maria Blancanales underwent rehabilitation treatment and counseling following her ordeal at Claudette Simms's

Wyoming ranch. Following a cross-country vacation that will include visiting her older sister Tony in New York, she plans to enroll for the fall semester at Pierce College and renew her plans to become an actress.

Pol Blancanales's right thigh still bothers him periodically, but he hasn't taken any time off for rest or relaxation since the events surrounding his film assignment on *You Ran, Iran*. However, he *has* taken the time to call home at least twice a month.

And Able Team?

Able Team is out there somewhere, right now, going head-to-head with the enemy, staying hard and doing what they know best.

As the countdown begins for the end of civilization,
America stands helpless at the mercy of the enemy
within.

DON PENDLETON's

MACK BOLAN

FIRE IN THE SKY

A conspiracy has taken root at the core of the U.S. military
when a fanatical group of Pentagon's elite prepare to fulfill
an ancient prophecy of ultimate destruction.

A secret arms deal
with Iran ignites a powder keg,
and a most daring mission is
about to begin.

THE BARRABAS STRIKE

JACK HILD

Nile Barrabas and his soldiers undertake a hazardous assignment when a powerful top-secret weapon disappears and shows up in Iran.
